I0667848

# The Culling

Charles Ray

North Potomac, MD

This book is a work of fiction. Names, descriptions, places, and incidents are products of the author's imagination, or are used fictionally. Any resemblance to actual events or persons, living or dead, is purely coincidental.

The reproduction or distribution, by any means, including electronic distribution, is expressly prohibited without the written consent of the copyright holder, except for fair use quotes in connection with reviews.

For information about this and other works of this author, contact the author at charlesray.author@yahoo.com.

Printed in the United States of America.

Copyright © 2013 Charles Ray

All rights reserved.

ISBN: 0615929192
ISBN-13: 978-0615929194 (Uhuru Press)

# DEDICATION

To Aldous Huxley (1894-1963) and George Orwell (1903-1950) who's writing set the standard for dystopian fiction. Huxley's *Brave New World*, published in 1932, which addressed psychological manipulation and operant conditioning, and how they impact social development, and Orwell's *1984*, in 1949, with its warning against Big Brother, might have been slightly off the mark in their predictions on the trajectory society was taking – but not by much. An avid reader from childhood, I was introduced to these two books at an age before I fully understood how society worked, but was nevertheless struck by how close they were to what a young country boy in segregated East Texas observed around him. Fiction doesn't have to get *all* the facts right to hit close to the *truth.*

**"Evil prevails when good men do nothing." – Aristotle**

***Cull.*** *v.t. 'to separate from others.'*

*n. 'anything selected from others; especially something inferior picked out and set apart.'*

## *Prologue*

When the end comes, will it be with a bang or with a whimper?

From the around the middle of the Twentieth Century, when the nations of the earth battled against each other, and two nations emerged from the ashes of the greatest conflict the earth had ever seen possessing enough weapons between them to obliterate all life on the planet many times over, this question was asked many times by many people. There were those who believed that one or the other of the two great powers, the United States of America, representing the so-called Free World, and the Soviet Union, representing the Communist World, would someday miscalculate and trigger a conflagration that would destroy humanity in a blaze of nuclear fire, leaving the planet's surface scorched and barren. Others felt that man's tendency to willfully ignore his impact on the planet's ecological balance would lead to a slow squeezing out of life, leaving the planet just as bare and sterile as a nuclear war.

The demise of one of the great powers, the Soviet Union, which suffered an economic and political collapse late in the century, somewhat allayed the fears of those who feared the end would come with a bang, but the continued pollution of the land, water, and air, continued to feed the angst of those who thought the end would be prolonged in coming, but would be no less final; who believed that irreversible changes were being made in the climate that would initiate geologic forces that would eventually reach a tipping point, triggering conditions that would make the planet uninhabitable, or at best, destroy the underpinnings of the global economy; leading to mass starvation and depopulation until it reached the point where humanity would first be plunged into a dark age of bare subsistence, and then, with a whimper, disappear.

Both, however, were wrong. Not about the end coming, but in what would bring it about.

Civilization ended, but it was with neither bang nor whimper.

Instead, it reeled, lurched, and staggered from crisis to crisis like a drunken man on a spree going from gin mill to gin mill, blind to the direction it was taking until, like the leaves of autumn that, one by one, disconnect from the boughs and fall aimlessly to the ground, leaving the trees bare, civilization's bones were laid bare, stripped of skin and muscle. It was process that, even when seen in retrospect, didn't signal clearly the final condition. One day though, the tree was bare.

That is how civilization ended; without a sound. One day it just wasn't there anymore.

At some time, in the far distant future, should some advanced race of alien archeologists visit this doomed planet, they will see the rusted and pitted signs of a great civilization, and they will wonder what caused it to disappear, to be replaced by small tribes of grimy, illiterate bipeds who cling precariously to life, but who have no higher purpose than survival from day to day. But, no matter how deep they dig, they will search in vain for an answer to that question, for there is no single answer, and it is unlikely that they will be able to communicate with the few bipeds left, for along with civilization, language will have been lost as well – or, language that carries meaning beyond 'danger,' 'food,' or the other single syllables of animals who eat, sleep, reproduce, and die. There are, however, many answers, but they don't fit together into any coherent narrative. The reasons for the decline were many. It was caused by forces that, unmindful of each other, worked in uncoordinated concert to precipitate an inexorable decline; a descent into an age that, while not quite dark, was cloaked in dimness.

Of all the factors contributing to civilization's demise, perhaps the most important two, because they created conditions that caused people who should have been aware to be ignorant of the other forces at work, was the unholy confluence of politics and religion – a marriage made in hell.

The religious factor had been at play for many years, dating perhaps from the very founding of organized religions, as there were always those who adopted a non-compromising view of religious doctrine, and insisted that theirs was the only valid doctrine, and all who failed to follow it were doomed to perdition – who often endeavored to assist 'non-believers' in achieving perdition through purges and massacres. In the late-Twentieth and early Twenty-first Centuries, the religious fundamentalists of all sects began to exert an inordinate amount of influence over the politics of their respective societies. An influence that extended into education, commerce, external relations, and eventually even family life, with disastrous consequences.

Religious fundamentalism would have been only a nuisance, though, had not a sense of fundamentalism taken hold in politics around the globe as well. Wars and economic upheaval created anxieties that gave political zealots an inordinate amount of influence in the halls of politics, especially in the industrialized countries where people saw their standard of living being eroded. When the political zealots met and made an uneasy alliance with the religious fundamentalists, the downward slide began in earnest.

The exact nature of this marriage of inconvenience varied from culture to culture, and from religion to religion, but all were characterized by strict adherence to whatever religious text the particular sect viewed as the 'container of the holy word,' and an extreme intolerance for divergent views. The impact was felt first; and perhaps most harshly, in education. Local institutions were pressured; at first by the religious leaders, but later by the political establishments as well; to teach only approved subjects. Books containing information that contradicted fundamentalist dogma were at first banned, and then later burned. Teachers who insisted upon academic freedom were shunned, dismissed from their positions, and in some cases either exiled or executed. The result was a generation of students whose education was warped to fit the views of those in charge, a disdain for independent academic inquiry, and erosion of scientific research. Teaching of evolution was banned in favor of religiously-based theories of mankind's origins, and research into climate change and its impact on the world's ecosystems came to a halt.

Whether religion influenced politics, or politics encouraged religion, the result was increased fragmentation between communities, a decrease in academic enquiry and scientific research, and an erosion of trust between people or in institutions outside those approved by the ruling cliques. Cross-border immigration, always a hot political issue, came to a virtual standstill, when many jurisdictions enacted harsh laws against illegal immigration, including in some places summary execution. Central governments began to break down as first state, and then local governments asserted more control over local affairs – and, local governments ceased to be servants of the population as order broke down, and became controllers in their misguided efforts to restore order and discipline. In some small countries, this led to open hostilities between central and local governments, but defections from central armies weakened the ability of bloated central bureaucracies to respond effectively.

Confined at first to the countries of the 'less developed' world, the fragmentation of world governments went unnoticed in the industrialized nations, who were busy dealing with their own local problems at the time. By the time the fragmentation effect began in the developed countries, it was too late.

The process of decline, which began in earnest in 2025, was essentially completed by 2035; in the space of a decade, nearly two thousand years of political, social, cultural, and scientific progress had not just been halted – it had been reversed. The great, and not so great, nation states disappeared. In their place there appeared a vast number of feudal communities, existing apart from each other in most cases, in reluctant and barely civil contact where geography made total separation impossible.

During this period of moral decay, nature was not still.

The decline in academic enquiry shut off all research into the potential deadly impact of climate change. At the same time, the loss of effective government control left the industrialists of the world, with their toxin-belching factories and insatiable greed for profit, free to rape the environment at will. The effect of greenhouse gases and pollution of air, soil and water increased to a tipping point; but, no one was paying attention until it was too late.

The production of greenhouse gases had been upsetting the earth's temperature for many decades, but when all government controls on industrial production were either lifted or ignored, it was no longer business as usual; it was rapine on a grand scale. By 2030, the regular average temperature worldwide had risen by ten degrees, and each year after that it got hotter by a degree. The melting of the polar ice caps, which increased the amount of water in the oceans, combined with the warmer temperatures which caused the water to expand, caused an average rise in sea levels of two meters globally. This took away some two hundred meters of shoreline from every coast, with high tides swamping most coastal cities, causing mass evacuations to inland locations and disruption of industry and commerce.

Seaports and coastal roads became unusable. Utilities such a water and power were disrupted, and the incidence of water borne and heat-related diseases rose dramatically. What few hospitals that remained open were quickly swamped. As food supplies, medicines, and other necessities became scarce, the crime rate skyrocketed. In a period of five years, law and order had broken down. People withdrew into small communities of the likeminded. Millions died, and with no one to bury them, corpses lay where they fell, further adding to disease.

By 2045, the surviving remnants of humanity had established a few thousand feudal communities scattered throughout the globe; out of touch with each other from a combination of loss of long-range communications technology, suspicion, and fear.

One such community, calling itself New Liberty, was established on the new east coast of what had been the United States of America; an area stretching from fifty miles south of the now inundated cities of Philadelphia, Pennsylvania and Wilmington, Delaware, southward to a point twenty miles north of Fredericksburg, Virginia.

In Washington, DC, the capital of the world's most powerful country, an alliance between political zealots and religious fundamentalists had been forged during the Twentieth Century, and as economic, social, and political crises increased in the late Twenty-First Century, this alliance deepened and was formalized in what became known as the People's Principles Party (PPP). While the party's public platform was a return to a literal interpretation of the U.S. Constitution, this was underpinned with an insistence on a literal interpretation of the King James Version of the Bible – said interpretation being validated and approved by the party's founder, Markham Christopher, an evangelist preacher who had run for and won a seat in the U.S. House of Representatives from a rural district in North Carolina. He was known for making public pronouncements of a coming Apocalypse, which would be divine punishment for all the sins humanity was committing in the name of science and progress. When the ocean moved in toward the west, wiping out coastal communities, large and small, it was seen as a vindication of Christopher's views.

As the world economic situation worsened, Christopher won more followers, and quickly became a kingmaker in what was left of national politics. When it became apparent that the sea levels were rising, threatening the 80% of the earth's population that lived in coastal areas, Christopher's gloom and doom predictions seemed validated. Christopher, though a fundamentalist zealot, was at heart a kind man, and the years under his rule were filled with hardships that were shared equally. When he died, though, he was replaced by Robert Cruz, owner of a chemical plant located in Delaware, just south of Wilmington. Not as kind-hearted as Christopher, he began to change community rules, establishing distinctions between workers and those for whom they worked. Under him, industrialists, as long as they hewed to the party line, ruled. It made the age of the nineteenth century robber barons of the railroads and mining interests seem mild. Workers became nothing more than replaceable economic units, whose only value was what they could produce for the bosses.

When Robert died in an unexplained bathroom accident, he was replaced in turn by his son Hector, who had been nothing but the heir apparent from birth. He continued what his father had begun, but under the tutelage of Elder Jebediah Robertson, a hard-core evangelist who had completely rewritten the King James Bible to reflect the coming of Apocalypse. He called his book, which was a perversion of Christopher's views, The Book of Apocalypse.

A ruling committee, consisting of Hector Cruz, Robertson, Minister of Defense Armand Wheelwright, Drake Edison, Minister of Population Control, and Colonel Gravius-One, commander of the New Liberty internal security unit, known as the Monitors, ran the affairs of the community with iron-fisted discipline.

The ruling committee, known only as The Committee, members of the elite citizen community, which included members of the new clergy and those who controlled production, designated full citizens, moved across the swollen Potomac River into what had been Rosslyn, Virginia. The Committee had its headquarters in the Pentagon, formerly the headquarters of the American defense forces, now the dreaded seat of power over everyone in New Liberty.

The rest of the population lived on the east side of the river in the former capital city, mostly in what had been low-income high rise buildings that had, since the collapse, become even more squalid. Overcrowding, disease, and crime were at first endemic. But, Edison, working with Gravius-One and his Monitors, moved to restore order. Despite his best efforts, though, Edison was unable to keep the people, now known as proles, from doing what impoverished people had been doing for ages, to relieve the tedium of their poverty, they procreated. The prole population doubled during the first five years, putting a strain on already limited resources. Edison then made a recommendation, which Cruz was all too willing to implement, and which was also supported by Robertson; new laws were passed making a long list of hitherto minor crimes, such as petty theft, having children without permission, and the like, capital offenses. Executions were carried out immediately after sentence was passed. While this did lower the population, it wasn't enough to stem the drain on food, which the proles were forced to grow and transfer the major part across the river to the citizens. The prole community was left with just enough to keep energy levels sufficient for their labor. Malnutrition was common, and most proles went to bed hungry at night.

It was in the sixth year after Hector Cruz assumed the office of Chairman of the Committee that the culling started. No record was made of the meeting at which this procedure was decided, but rumors circulated that it was a joint idea of the good Elder Robertson and Minister Edison. Each year, those in the population who reached the age of nineteen would be evaluated for their potential for contributing to society. Those with no skills, or who were chronic misbehavers, were placed with the convicted criminals who were scheduled for execution – and, this was almost all convicted criminals. The selected ones were then taken to the Culling Ground, the area that had been known as the National Mall, where they were placed in a cleared area near the obelisk that thrust up like a misshapen phallus in the center of the area, under the watchful eye of a unit of Monitors. The prole community would be ordered to assemble to observe the process; those who could not find space near the Culling Ground were required to watch on television monitors at their places of work.

A device that was located at the top of the obelisk would be aimed at them. At the stroke of midday, a yellow light would emanate from the opening at the top of the obelisk, bathing the assembled prisoners below. At first, they would stumble around in confusion, but very quickly the searing pain would start, and someone would scream. But, before they could flee the unbearable agony, there would be a flash, and the stench of burning flesh and billowing smoke would fill the air. After a few minutes the smoke would clear, but the odor would linger, often for days. In the clearing at the base of the obelisk, where only moments before living, breathing human beings stood, were piles of gray ash, which work gangs of proles would be ordered in to rake up, place in baskets and take to the agricultural fields to be spread as fertilizer.

As the workers cleared the ash, the nasal tone of The Chairman would issue from the loudspeakers that were placed at intervals throughout the prole community, "Dear people, residents of New Liberty, yet again those who have put their own selfish needs above those of the community have paid the price for that selfishness. They are finally contributing to the community in a meaningful way. May peace be with you."

As the last of the ashes were cleared, proles made their way back to their hovels, most, happy that this year they had not been selected for culling. Those looking at their nineteenth year coming, wondering if their names would be on the list at the next event. Heads bowed, not speaking, not making eye contact with the person standing next to them, for fear that they might be looking at someone scheduled to become one with the earth.

The monitors, other than those assigned security and patrol duty in the community, formed ranks and marched back across the river.

# 1.

## *2072 AD/18 A.A. – New Liberty*

## *Columbus Heights Crèche*

"Mr. Jefferson, you are not paying attention," the stentorian tones of Octavia Olympus, head of the Columbus Heights Crèche, yanked Hiroshi Jefferson from his reverie.

With her orange hair piled high atop her narrow head, her grayish-orange complexion, and the dull-green one-piece dress draped over her skinny frame, she looked like some of the vegetables Hiroshi had to harvest from the fields to the west of the crèche, where he spent the time when he wasn't working, in the company of two hundred other children ranging in age from newborn infant to Hiroshi's eighteen years. He'd been a resident of Columbus

Heights since just before he turned seven, unlike the others who had been placed there immediately after birth, and had never quite adapted to the norms of behavior expected of crèche residents. While Olympus found his behavior disruptive, she also found herself often drawn to him – an attraction she could not explain.

“Sorry, Miss Olympus,” he said without a trace of sincerity. “I’m still tired I guess. They had us working late yesterday harvesting potatoes.” That, at least, was true. His work crew hadn’t been allowed to return to the crèche until well after sunset.

“You are to address me as headmaster, Mr. Jefferson,” she said. Hiroshi could feel the chill in her voice. She looked around the room at the other students who sat alert, their bright eyes on her. “Your sector mates had to work late as well, but I don’t see them daydreaming.”

“Yes, headmaster,” he said, looking away from her piercing gaze. As his head turned, he caught the eye of his best friend, Washington Benedict, also eighteen, who sat across the crowded classroom from him.

Washington, his dark brown face impassive, returned his gaze. Then, his full lips twitched up slightly and he slowly closed his left eye. This was as much as he dared do to support his friend’s rebelliousness, but for Hiroshi it was enough.

The two boys had been friends from the day that Hiroshi had been taken from his parents and transported to Columbus Heights. Washington, who had been in the crèche since birth, had never known his own parents, and as a consequence was curious about Hiroshi, who had spent so much time with a mother and father rather than the impersonal crèche attendants. For Hiroshi, it had been a way to retain the memory of his own parents as he and Washington sneaked from their cots at night when the attendants were less attentive, and talked for hours in a darkened storage closet at the back of the sleeping room where fifty children were housed.

As time went on, what had begun out of curiosity had developed into a close bond. The two boys became as close as blood brothers ever could. They were inseparable, and at the age of ten had sworn oaths of loyalty. Washington was fascinated by Hiroshi's stories of a life that he'd never known, and Hiroshi kept alive the memory of his mother, Junko, a tiny woman with delicate features and a musical laugh, and his father Ulysses, a mountain of a man, with skin the color of mahogany, who, despite his immense strength, was as gentle as a spring breeze.

Hiroshi had inherited his mother's delicate features and size, and his father's physical strength and indomitable will, which in the regimented environment of the crèche, where conformity and immediate obedience were the first two rules, meant that he was constantly in trouble, even from the beginning.

“Tell me, Mr. Jefferson,” Olympus said, looming over Hiroshi, her orange hair blocking the light from the grim-spattered window. “What is the first rule of the community?”

Hiroshi took a deep breath. He regarded the headmaster levelly, his dark brown almond-shaped eyes not betraying the emotions that raged beneath the surface. The only sign of his anger, and only his friend Washington noticed this, was the two faint circles of red that blossomed on his light brown cheeks.

“The first rule of the community,” he said quietly. “Is that the needs of the community come before the needs of the individual.”

His gaze locked with Olympus. A muscle in her cheek twitched. This was the one student; she thought of them as students rather than inmates, which was how they thought of themselves; that she could not fathom. He was intelligent, far more so than any of the others, but he had a stubborn streak that she could not understand. Finally, when she could take it no longer, she wrenched her gaze away.

“Very good . . . Mr. Jackson,” she said, struggling to maintain control of her voice. She glanced at the chrono on her wrist; nearly lunch hour. She breathed a sigh of relief; an hour away from that boy and those piercing eyes. "That will be all, children. You may go to lunch now."

She almost fled from the room.

"I don't think the headmaster likes you," Washington said as they walked shoulder to shoulder toward the canteen.

"Well, the feeling is mutual," Hiroshi said. "I especially hate the way she treats us like animals in a zoo."

"What's a zoo?"

"You forget already, Wash? I told you; a zoo was a place where they kept all the animals in cages, and people would go and look at them."

"Oh, yeah, I remember now," Washington said. "Wow, Hirosh, where'd you learn stuff like that?"

Although his parents' faces were dimly remembered after nearly eleven years, the one memory that was clear in Hiroshi's mind was that of the times his father had taken him to the secret place near their residence, the place of the books. He remembered his father reading to him from the thick, dusty volumes, reading of strange places and fascinating people and events. Most clear, though, was his father's warning: "You must never ever tell anyone of this place, Hiroshi. The Committee doesn't know it wasn't destroyed in the great purge. If they discover it, all of this knowledge will die, and anyone associated with it will be killed."

A young Hiroshi didn't understand his father's warning at first. But, when the black-uniformed Monitors, their faces masked by dark visors, came to take his mother and father away, and transport him to the crèche, he understood. The Monitors worked for The Committee; the shadowy body on the other side of the turgid, brown waters of the forbidden river that ruled their lives; a body that had the power of life and death over those living in New Liberty. He had never spoken of the place of books to anyone, not even his friend Washington.

"My father used to tell me stories," he said. "They still had zoos, and libraries and stuff like that when he was a boy."

As they entered the line of boys and girls waiting to enter the dining facility, they lowered their voices. Not that anyone was paying them any attention, but they'd learned to be cautious with their conversations over the years.

"I remember libraries," Washington said. "You said that was a place where they kept books, and people could go and read them, right?"

"That's right." Hiroshi nodded and patted his

friend's shoulder. "You could even borrow books to take home."

"You're making that up." Washington's eyes went round. In his world, there were only a few books, the Book of Apocalypse, which was required reading for every prole in New Liberty who'd past the age of ten, and the instruction manuals for the machines proles used in their work; most of the latter were primarily pictures, with text only when an operation couldn't be adequately portrayed in the cartoon-like pictures. None of these, however, could be removed from the crèche reading room, and could only be read under the watchful eye of the headmaster or one of the attendants. The idea that an individual could actually possess a book, and read it unsupervised, was alien to him.

"I am not," Hiroshi insisted. "That's what my father told me, and my father never lied."

Washington could only shake his head. His friend had indeed had an incredible childhood, or he was the best storyteller Washington had ever seen.

Near the entrance the line slowed as attendants checked the name of each child entering. Beyond the double-wide door frame, they could hear the disembodied female voice that sounded so much like Headmaster Olympus coming over the loudspeakers set at intervals around the walls inside the dining facility, *"The good of the community is superior to the good of the individual. The highest achievement of the individual is to contribute to the community."* These, and similar, slogans were heard everywhere within the crèche except the classrooms, where attendants did little else but spout them. The announcements began at first light and continued until lights out. Hiroshi had learned to tune them out.

"What mischief are you two up to?" a cheerful voice said from behind them.

Clementine Adams squeezed between the two boys and linked her arms with theirs. While Washington towered over her five-two form, Hiroshi's height had come from his mother; he was only three inches taller. Where the two boys were dark, her skin was as pale as fine porcelain. She had an oval face, a small, turned up nose above lips that were naturally red and always smiling. Her light blue eyes also seemed to smile.

She had, like Washington, been taken from her parents at birth and raised in the crèche. But, unlike Washington's parents, who had been mere laborers, Clementine's father ran the largest dry good store in the prole community, which enabled the Adams family to get visitation rights. They could meet with their only child for one hour each month, under the supervision of one of the crèche attendants. At no time during the visits were they allowed to identify themselves as her parents, a strange situation at first, but by the time Clementine was ten she'd figured out who they were anyway – she continued, however, to play the game, pretending that these two nice people were just members of the prole community who liked spending time with children. She was one of a very few children in the crèche who were entitled to visits, so it hadn't been hard to figure it out.

Like Washington, she'd been fascinated by Hiroshi. He'd actually spent his first seven years with a mother and father, in a family. In addition, she found his small, muscular frame and dark good looks fascinating; more so as they reached puberty. Hiroshi hadn't noticed her at first as anything other than in interesting friend, but he too, as the hormonal rush of puberty hit him, noticed that she was interesting in other ways as well. He knew that Washington had also noticed the way her hips had started flaring from her narrow waist, and how the top half of the singlet she wore protruded in different ways than his own did.

Having been raised in the sterile environment of the crèche, though, none of them truly understood the conflicting emotions they felt. The only thing they knew for certain was that they were friends and that as friends they had to stick together. As was their usual practice, they found a table in the far corner of the meal room, somewhat away from the others, and after getting trays containing the gray, unrecognizable mass that passed for food, retired to 'their' corner.

"Okay, you two," Clementine said as she frowned down at the lumpy food on the plastic plate. "You didn't answer my question; what were you two talking about?"

Washington shoved a spoonful of the gunk into his mouth, wrinkled his nose, chewed a few times and then swallowed, making a gulping noise.

"Eeyew, this stuff tastes worse every meal," he said. He took a drink of tepid water from his plastic cup. "Hirosh was telling me this tall tale about places called libraries, where people could go and get books to read."

"It wasn't a tall tale," Hiroshi insisted. "Honest, Clem, my father told me there were places like that, and my father would never lie to me."

Clementine looked at Hiroshi, her eyes wide.

"Your father was born in the time before, right?"

"Of course," Hiroshi said. "I was born in Year One." He turned to Washington. "You were too, Wash. You and me, we're among the few people born in the first year of Apocalypse."

Clementine nodded.

"My paren-, er, the people who come visit me, were born in the time before, too. They don't talk about it, but I get a feeling they remember things like that. I believe you Hiroshi. It was different in the time before."

"See, Clem believes me," Hiroshi said. "It's true, too."

Washington shook his head.

"Wow! That must have been something. I mean, being able to read anything you wanted to read."

*"Learning is useful only if it serves the community,"* the disembodied voice said, as if it had heard Washington's remark.

The three of them giggled, covering their mouths to try and avoid attracting too much attention.

Then, as they looked around, their eyes went wide. An attendant, dressed in a singlesuit, the same dull green color as the dress Olympus wore, only with pants that clung to her, as both Hiroshi and Washington noticed, shapely legs, was heading their way. The effect of her shapely form was ruined by the boys by the dull look in her blue eyes. All of the attendants had blue eyes, and they all had the uninterested expressions of sleepwalkers.

It was clear that she was coming to their table. Hiroshi wondered if maybe they'd been talking too loud and been overheard. If so, they'd be in trouble for engaging in conversation about one of the forbidden subjects – books. In his early days, before he'd learned the taboos, he'd been punished often for talking about things that were banned; books, families, individual activities. He'd learned, though, to keep such things to himself, or to discuss them quietly with the only two people he could trust, Clementine and Washington.

His heart was pounding so when the attendant stopped at their table, he was sure she could hear it. He held his breath.

"Mr. Jackson, Mr. Benedict," she said in that boring, droning voice that all the attendants had. "I have your work assignments for the afternoon.

Hiroshi let out his breath.

"You will report to the animal area where you will clean out the pig and chicken enclosures immediately at the end of the meal period."

Her duty done, the attendant spun on her heels and silently glided across the dining facility toward the exit.

Washington and Clementine were making sour faces.

"I think maybe I'll eat supper alone," Clementine said, pinching her nostrils together. "And, maybe even breakfast tomorrow."

"Aw, come on; it's not really that bad," Washington said. But, there was no conviction in his voice. "Besides, that new cedar scent disinfectant they have in the bath unit is pretty good."

"Yeah," Hiroshi chimed in. "It makes you smell like pig manure in a cedar forest. If I could avoid being around me after shoveling pig shit for four hours, I would."

Washington shrugged and laughed.

"And, the chicken pens aren't much better."

*"To work diligently for the benefit of the community benefits all."*

## 2.

### *The Committee*

Across the turgid brown waters of the forbidden river, formerly known as the Potomac, nestled amid a tangled profusion of lush green trees and vines, sits a massive five-sided structure. The mottled grey concrete walls are covered in gnarled vines of English ivy that cling like great green snakes, covering the fly-specked windows. The wide expanse around the building, once parking lots for thousands of vehicles, was now broken slabs of concrete covered with trees and vines, with narrow paths cut through leading to the high-rise buildings to the north and south.

The building, which once housed over 30,000 workers, was now home to the members of The Committee of New Liberty, their immediate families, aides, security guards, and retainers who served their every need. The only exception was Gravius-One, commander of the monitors, who had his residence in a one-story brick building, a few hundred yards away, from where he oversaw the activities of several hundred black-clad monitors.

From the second floor to the top of the headquarters were the residences, dining facilities, hospital, stores, and schools that served the elite of New Liberty's citizens; those permitted to live west of the forbidden river. Residents of the building were the ruling elite, while the managers, caretakers, security forces, and attendants who oversaw the proles living to the east of the river, behind barriers and a razor-sharp fence, whose labor provided the clothing, food, and tools used by citizens, lived in high-rise buildings to the north and south. The building, like New Liberty itself, was encircled by a twelve-foot-high fence topped with razor wire, and guarded by black-suited Monitors; specially selected members of the security force. The ground floor contained administrative offices to which citizens with special passes could go to submit petitions, answer summons, or receive instructions. Below this were two subterranean floors, to which only the high ranking members of The Committee and specially-assigned Monitors were granted admittance.

In a special room in the lowest basement, a circular room with large monitor screens on the walls, seated around a large circular table, the members of The Committee met on a weekly basis, or when called by the Chairman.

A guard, dressed in a shiny black singlesuit, and wearing a black ceramic helmet with the Plexiglas one-way visor pulled down, making his face invisible, stood alert at the door, as unmoving as an obsidian statue. Clipped to the waist of his singlesuit was a large, black, evil-looking flechette gun, a weapon that spit out a thousand tiny lethal metal darts per second, reducing a human target to so much shredded meat. A twin of the guard stood outside the door. Any authorized individual approaching the door from outside would be challenged at fifty feet, and eliminated at twenty-five.

It was the middle of the week, not a normal meeting day, and the members were seated, awaiting the arrival of the Chairman, each wondering at the reason for this special, unscheduled meeting.

While a round table can't be said to have a head, the presence of an empty chair, more opulent and high-backed than the rest, at the point of the circle nearest the entrance, marked the position of that individual at the table who was first among equals. Flanking that empty chair, in the order of their perceived rank from its occupant, were the members of New Liberty's Ruling Committee, which was known to all merely as The Committee.

To the right of the empty chair sat Elder Jebediah Robertson, spiritual advisor to the Chairman and Minister of Religious and Social Affairs. A tall, thin man, with pale, mottled flesh drawn tight over his narrow face, and lank, brown hair that was thinning and revealing dark liver spots on his skull. His cadaverous appearance was matched with a dour expression.

To the left sat Robertson's principal rival for the attention of the Chairman. A rotund, balding man with perpetually pursed lips, and watery blue eyes, Drake Edison was Minister of Population Control. He hated Robertson for his influence over the Chairman, influence he thought should be his, and only his, to wield.

To Edison's left was Armand Wheelwright, a broad-shouldered man with steel-gray hair and a square jaw, whose almond-shaped eyes and high cheekbones were the only signs of his Asian and Native American ancestry. Wheelwright was New Liberty's Minister of Defense, a position that had been important in the early days of the community, but as communities became increasingly isolated and wary of contact with each other his only role was the protection of the community from infrequent raids from barbarians from the wild country outside the community. Poorly armed, the Wild Ones, as they were called, stood little chance against his forces.

A man dressed entirely in black, with skin only a few shades lighter than his uniform, sat next to Wheelwright. Piercing brown eyes glared at the world from beneath a slightly protruding, wide forehead. Slightly fleshy lips beneath the flaring nostrils of a broad nose gave Gravius-One, Commander of the Monitors, New Liberty's internal security arm, the look of someone who had smelled something distasteful.

Completing the circle, sitting between Gravius and Robertson was a gray man. Nigel Halifax, the head of research for New Liberty, had rumpled gray hair that raggedly framed a gray oval face. He wore a collarless gray tunic over wrinkled gray pants, and his black shoes were always covered with a thin layer of gray dust. He never spoke during meetings, keeping his eyes fixed on the notebook he kept on the table before him.

Except for the hum of the ventilation units, and the occasional scraping sound of a shoe on the hard linoleum floor, the room was silent. The five men sitting there had little to say to each other. They, in fact, detested each other, each for his own unique reason. These men, in fact, knew only two emotions; hate for each other, and fear of the Chairman.

All heads snapped around toward the door when the guard suddenly moved to the side and pivoted to open it.

Hector Cruz, Chairman of The Committee, first among equals in the elite group that ruled New Liberty and everyone within its borders, strode confidently into the room. That he had kept them waiting for over an hour didn't bother him. He was, after all, the Chairman. His, and only his, time was important and precious. He glanced indifferently around the circle of blank, waiting faces, his amber eyes as lifeless as stone.

He was neither slender nor fat, neither tall nor short. In fact, except for the amber color of his eyes, Hector Cruz was an unremarkable individual. He was dressed in a plain brown singlesuit, devoid of any insignia of rank. He could walk among the citizens of New Liberty unnoticed until you looked into his amber eyes. The lack of emotion reflected there usually stopped in their tracks. Looking into his eyes was like looking at two polished pieces of stone. Your reflection bounced back from the hard, unyielding surface, beneath which there was nothing.

With measured pace, Cruz walked to his place at the table. He stood there for several heartbeats, his head moving slowly from left to right, looking at, no looking into, each man there. Each man kept his gaze steadily on the table in front of him, but each could feel the frigid sweep of that steely scan. Finally, Cruz sat.

"Well, citizens," he said in a voice that was as cold and emotionless as his gaze. "Thank you for your presence today." As if their presence was voluntary. "I know this is not a normally scheduled meeting day, and that each of you has important work to do, but there are things that concern me that I feel I needs must consult you on."

Four heads tilted up – Nigel Halifax continued to study the pad in front of him – four pairs of eyes questioning. Robertson finally broke the silence.

"What could that be, Citizen Cruz?" he asked. "Production levels are within normal parameters; there have been no reports of Wild One activity on our borders; what can there be to be concerned about?"

The others held their collective breaths. Only Robertson among them would dare to speak in a manner that seemed to contradict Cruz. But, even he was not completely immune from Cruz's occasional fits of temper. And, one thing that was usually guaranteed to provoke an outburst was being disagreed with, or to hear words that even distantly implied that he might be anything but right.

Cruz looked at Robertson like a crocodile watching a young, succulent animal that has wandered too close to the river. Then, his thin lips turned up a fraction of a millimeter – what on his face passed for a smile. Four sets of lungs let air seep out slowly.

"That, my dear citizen, is because you fail to look behind the numbers. You see only what's reported; so many acres planted, so many metric tons harvested. It's what you can't see that you must be truly concerned about."

While the others looked on, questions in their eyes, Robertson smiled back at the man who held the lives of so many in his hands. He'd heard this before; during his private spiritual development sessions with the Chairman. He inclined his head in a slight bow.

"And, what is it behind the numbers that we should be aware of?" he asked, putting just a touch of deference in his voice. He knew that Cruz liked that.

"We are allowing the seed of rebellion,

planted at birth, to grow unimpeded within our very midst. For more than a decade now, that seed has no doubt infected others."

It was, Robertson feared, the first sign of mental and emotional decline. For several weeks not, in their sessions, Cruz had begun to ramble about some event that had occurred ten years previously; an event that had doubtlessly shaken him, but had until now been repressed. He would never be specific, only ramble about an *unfinished* task; one that it might yet even be too late to accomplish.

Robertson saw the frowns of curiosity on the others' faces. Even if he'd wanted to share with them; and, he didn't; the sanctity of the spiritual confession had to be respected. It said no less in the Book of Apocalypse, and he lived by the Book.

"Perhaps if you could give us the identity of this seed, we could take care of it," he said.

Cruz seemed to snap back to focus, to return from some place that only he knew. His hard amber eyes bored through Robertson.

"No, citizen," he said. "This is something that I must do. I called you together today, though, to discuss something else. As you know, there will be a Culling soon. I propose that we change the rules to allow culling of proles under the age of nineteen."

Robertson's eyebrows rose. This, too, was a conversation he and Cruz had had; one that they vehemently disagreed on. The Book of Apocalypse was specific on that point; the punishment of society could only be applied to those who had reached the age of maturity, nineteen according to the Book. On this issue, he knew he could rebut the mercurial Cruz with impunity. Not even the Chairman would openly defy the Word.

"But, citizen," Robertson said. "The Book of Apocalypse says that only those who have reached maturity can be culled. To go against the Word is to invite divine retribution."

Cruz cleared his throat, looking down at the table.

"I can't believe the Book would disagree with an action that could ensure the continued survival of the community, elder." The use of his title, rather than 'citizen,' told Robertson that he'd struck a nerve. "There has to be an exception in extraordinary circumstances," Cruz said defensively.

"What extraordinary circumstances?" asked Drake Edison. "Food production is within required norms."

"There have been no raids by the Wild Ones," Armand Wheelwright chimed in.

"And, we've had no incidents of violence, and very few thefts, for the past several weeks," Gravius-One added.

Cruz looked at each of them, his face a study in disdain.

"I really don't think you're prepared to understand." He turned toward the door. "I'm thirsty. Monitor, please bring me a glass of water."

The black-suited guard walked to the credenza beneath the large, inert screen. He picked up a large crystal pitcher of water and poured into a tumbler that sat next to the pitcher on a silver tray. He picked up the tumbler and started toward the Chairman's position.

What happened next was not clear, nor was it ever adequately explained. As the man carrying the tumbler of water approached the chairman, Robertson turned in his chair, his long legs thrusting outward. The guard's right foot bumped Robertson's leg, throwing his balance off. His arms shot forward in a reflex action, causing the water in the tumbler to slosh over the rim, splashing into Cruz's face.

Hector Cruz's face contorted in shock and anger as the water dripped from his chin onto his clothing, leaving dark brown blotches in the shiny fabric.

Seeing the expression on Cruz's face, the monitor backed up, his body quivering.

"S-sorry, citizen," he said. "It w-was an accident."

Cruz rose from his seat. His body too was quivering, but from rage rather than fear.

"What is your designation, monitor?" He asked; his voice as hard as tempered steel.

"L-leland-27, citizen."

"Well, Leland-27, you are a member of the elite guard of the Monitors, are you not?"

"Y-yes, citizen."

"So, that means you've had special training; that you are among the best of the best?"

"Y-yes, citizen; I was f-first in my training class."

Cruz made a snorting sound.

"Well, either the training is deficient, monitor, or you have forgotten your training. Remove your visor. I wish to see your face."

The man touched a button at the side of his helmet. The visor retracted upwards, revealing a clean shaven face, light blue eyes, an aquiline nose, and a broad forehead. There was a look of fear in the young man's eyes.

Cruz turned to Gravius-One.

“I want this man executed immediately as an object lesson to the rest of your *elite* guards that I will not tolerate sloppiness in this facility.”

Gravius-One’s face hardened as he rose to face Cruz.

“If I may, citizen,” he said. “While I agree that an example should be made, I would like to offer an even more fitting punishment, if I may.”

“What, Citizen Gravius, is more fitting than death?”

The monitor commander’s fleshy lips curled up into a macabre smile; slightly parted, they revealed two rows of brilliant white teeth.

“Death, citizen, is final. People soon forget the dead. If, on the other hand, the punishment is something that goes on and on, and is there for all to see, does it not have a more long-lasting effect?”

Cruz looked at the dark man for a moment, and then smiled.

“I do see your point. But then, that is why I kept you on commander of the monitors after my fa-, the previous Chairman died – you have a wonderfully devious mind. What do you have in mind?"

"Other than sentry duty at the animal enclosures, the most distasteful and dangerous duty is the external patrol in the west. We lose two or three men a year out there to barbarian raids, which is why it is duty usually restricted to one month each year for monitors. I should think that being permanently assigned to the western frontier would be a punishment that is worse than death."

Cruz laughed; a mirthless, evil sound that made Leland-27's body feel cold.

"I do believe I like your punishment much more than mine. Once again, Gravius, you please me greatly. Make it so." He turned to the others. "I'm a bit exhausted by this turn of events, citizens. We can take this up again at out next meeting. You are excused." As the four remaining men rose, Cruz raised a pale hand. "Not you, Citizen Halifax. I have a matter that I must discuss with you alone."

Halifax, his face even grayer, sat back down. The others filed quietly out. Cruz sat in the chair vacated by Robertson and leaned close until his face was almost touching the other man's.

"What have you to report, Citizen

Halifax?"

For the first time, Nigel Halifax met Cruz's gaze.

Now, preparing to discuss his research, Halifax was in his comfort zone. He ran a hand through his rumpled hair.

"We have had some minor success with the life-extending research, citizen. A few more months of testing, and I believe it will be ready." He opened his notebook. "We only have to work on the side effects, but I'm confident that we will solve that problem soon.

The gray-clad little man opened the notebook that he'd been staring at throughout the previous meeting. Barely legible, spidery writing covered the yellowed pages.

"The, uh, special project you requested that I work on," Halifax continued. "Has run into, uh, a little snag . . . I'm having difficulty developing a targeting system that will key on a specific person."

"But, you assured me you could do it," Cruz said with menace in his voice.

"Oh, I can, and I will. It's just that . . . working on it alone . . . well, it's rather complicated, and I must oversee the other work as well. That and the lack of proper texts means that it will take me a bit longer than I originally anticipated."

"Do not disappoint me, Citizen Halifax."

Halifax looked up. A slight hint of color appeared in his grayish cheeks.

"Have I ever disappointed you, citizen?" There was challenge in his voice. "It might take longer than planned, but I have *always* delivered what I promise. Now, as to your last major project of interest; there is one issue that my people are at odds about that requires your decision."

"What is that?" Cruz asked coldly.

"On the matter of controlling the prole population; the behaviorists on my staff prefer psychological conditioning from birth, while the chemists believe we could achieve the level of submissiveness we desire with carefully spaced chemical injections."

"I have you on The Committee to advise me on such matters," Cruz said. "Which method do you think will be most effective?"

"Both have strengths and weaknesses. While the chemical method is quicker, individuals with high tolerance can be unaffected unless given dosages high enough to be potentially fatal. The conditioning method takes longer, but is at the subconscious level, making it a very powerful motivator. My own preference, though, would be conditioning from birth, augmented with chemical injections at the onset of puberty. The chemicals, given at a time of major hormonal activity, would cement the conditioning, resulting in adult proles who would only think one way, and who would be completely satisfied with their assigned slot in life."

Cruz smiled his vulpine smile. The thought of a population of workers, strong, healthy, but completely docile; workers who would do the basest of jobs and enjoy them, accept them as their due, gave him a feeling of warmth like nothing else ever could. With the prole population approaching a number that would put strains on food production, and a citizen population approaching the limits of The Committee's ability to keep them employed and entertained, he had come up with an idea that would ensure the continued existence of New Liberty, but in a form that no one before him had dared contemplate. And, leading the community into this new Eden would be its First Citizen, Hector Cruz.

"Very well, citizen," he said. "Go back and encourage your people to redouble their efforts."

Snatching up his notebook, the gray man scurried from the room.

# 3.

For five minutes after Halifax had departed, Hector Cruz sat in his high-backed chair, staring at the ceiling and listening to the hum of the air circulation system.

As often happened when Cruz was alone, his mind drifted back nearly twenty years to the time before he ascended to the position of Chairman of The Committee. As son of the Chairman, it was expected that he would replace his father, but while he waited – impatiently - he spent much of his time with his best friend, Ulysses Jackson, who was a minor official in the Ministry of Population Control.

The two had met when Jackson first came to the west side of the river, a teenage orphan whose parents had been file clerks in the Library of Congress during the time of the purge. When mobs led by the newly formed

Monitor organization stormed the library to burn the forbidden texts, the Jacksons, Benjamin and Elizabeth, trying to protect what they regarded as a treasured storehouse of mankind's knowledge, had been killed. The young Ulysses, at home during the tragic incident, had been taken in by Hector's father and raised in the Cruz household, becoming in effect Hector's foster brother.

The two boys were very different. Hector, pale and undernourished, was the polar opposite of Ulysses, with his caramel colored skin and athletic build. While Hector preferred spending his time at one of the never-ending parties that took place among the citizenry, who, unless they supervised a factory in the prole community had little else to do, Benjamin spent his time either studying from the few surviving books that were only permitted west of the river, or playing sports with the few boys who were so inclined. They were, nonetheless, as close as if they shared the same bloodline.

There were only two areas of real contention between them; while Hector cared little about the plight of the proles, thinking of them only as economic units whose sole purpose was to provide the goods and services that citizens demanded, Ulysses constantly spoke of the need to treat them as human beings entitled to the same things in life as everyone else. He objected to the distinction between 'citizen' and 'prole,' and as he grew older, frequently clashed with the hierarchy over his refusal to use the title citizen when referring to others. The other area of conflict was Junko Miyako, a petite girl of their age, who shared classes with them. Both had fallen madly in love with her, and for a time, she was torn between the two. Hector, she knew, would someday be Chairman, and to be associated with him guaranteed her position at the top of the pyramid of citizenry. Ulysses, on the other hand, was handsome and caring, traits she valued highly.

In the end, caring won out; which led to a final confrontation between the two men shortly after they turned twenty-one?

The three were together on the vine-covered terrace at the east side of the large pentagonal building that housed The Committee. The sun was setting in the west, casting long shadows over the foliage-choked area from there to the river, and the pall of smog from the factories to the east, gave an orange cast to the cloud. The smell of methane generators, the sole remaining source of power for New Liberty, was light in the air, thanks to a wind blowing from the east.

Hector and Ulysses were arguing again about whether or not proles should have the same rights as citizens, while Junko stood silently by watching them, a half smile on her oval face.

"Not only should they have the *same* rights," Ulysses insisted. "But, they are citizens just the same as you and me."

Hector laughed harshly.

"How can you say that, Ulysses? Look at them; they're ignorant and mostly unclean. You can't possibly think of a prole as your equal."

"They are not ignorant, just uneducated; and that's because we make it unlawful for them to learn anything but what they need to know to do their assigned jobs. As to being unclean, I'd like to see how clean you'd be if you had to live in such crowded squalor," Ulysses said. His brown face was contorted in anger. "We don't ensure they have the same access to clean water that we do, and even though they run the power plant which keeps us well lit and cool with our air circulation units, they live in crowded spaces with only a bare bulb for light – when the current even works in their buildings."

"Don't you understand? They wouldn't be made happy if their heads were filled with useless information. It would, in fact, only frustrate them. The proles are meant to serve, and as to the crowded squalor, if they were not such prolific procreators, they wouldn't be so crowded."

"They have little else to do for recreation," Junko said. Both men turned toward her.

"Junko," Hector said. "That is hardly the type of language that should be coming from your mouth."

Ulysses smiled.

"She does make a point, though," he said. "The proles labor from sunup to sundown, and are constantly bombarded with propaganda slogans about working for the good of the community. Yet, they see none of the good from their work for themselves. When the sun goes down, what else is there for them to do? My father used to say, not completely in jest, 'the rich get richer, while the poor make babies.' I never understood it until now."

Hector's face reddened. For all his pursuits of debauchery, he was uncomfortable having such a conversation in Junko's presence, especially so as she'd been the one to broach the subject.

"So, brother, what would you have us do about it?" he asked, changing the subject. "Maybe we should sterilize them, or make it illegal for proles of different sexes to occupy the same space. Hell, as long as they produce enough future workers, I don't see why we shouldn't introduce breeding control programs."

Ulysses faced him, staring deeply into his face. He knew Hector wasn't joking. At that moment, he wanted nothing more than to smash his foster brother's face. Instead, he would smash his inflated ego.

"You know I've spoken of returning to the prole community many times. Well, I've decided; now that I'm an adult and can make my own decisions, I will go back and do what I can do to improve living conditions among the proles."

Hector, shocked at the vehemence in Ulysses's voice, stepped back.

"I always thought that was just so much gas. You can't be serious."

Ulysses placed a hand on his shoulder.

"I am quite serious. I'm leaving at first light as a matter of fact."

While Hector would miss his foster brother, one part of his mind was elated. With Benjamin gone, there would be no more competition for Junko's attention and affection.

"You . . . you've received The Committee's permission?"

"I have. They were reluctant at first, but when they realized that I was adamant, they gave in."

"You're giving up your citizenship? For what? To live in squalor?"

"What is that slogan? Oh yes, 'for the good of the community.' I'll miss you, Hector."

"And, I'll miss you too, brother." There was no real sincerity in his voice as Hector moved near to Junko. "I guess you'll miss him too, eh, Junko?"

She turned her gaze away from his, looking out over the river.

"Junko, what is it?" he asked.

"I'm sorry, Hector, but . . . I have decided to go with Ulysses."

Hector Cruz paled. His mouth fell open. He stared first at Junko, and then at Ulysses. His mouth snapped shut and turned down in an angry snarl.

"You . . . you talked her into this craziness, didn't you?"

"No, Hector," Junko said. "It was my idea. I believe in what Ulysses is doing, and I want to help."

"You, you can't do this."

She put her hands at her tiny waist and glared up at Hector.

"I can do what I chose to do, Hector Cruz," she said. "And, I've decided this is what I chose to do."

Hector turned on Ulysses, his face now red, tears in his eyes.

"I'll never forgive you for this. One day, you'll pay for this." He glared at Junko. "One day you'll *both* regret this." He spun on his heels and walked away, his back straight, but with his head averted so they couldn't see the tears in his eyes.

*"You are a dead man, Ulysses Jackson, foster brother or no."*

## 4.

As the guard vehicle approached the razor-wire barrier in the middle of the north bridge over the forbidden river it slowed.

A helmeted driver and another helmeted monitor sat in the front. In back, Gravius-One and Leland-27 sat in silence, their visors pulled down.

Gravius thumbed a number pad worn on a strap around his left wrist. One of the few communications devices left from the time before things crashed, it sent an electronic pulse to a receiver that signaled to the gate that the commander was approaching. Ahead, the guards snapped to attention as the barrier began lifting. The Monitor commander's vehicle was recognized, and except for any vehicle transporting the Chairman, was the only conveyance in all of New Liberty that was not stopped at checkpoints. Since the Chairman never crossed the river into the prole community, Gravius's vehicle was the only one accorded such courtesies.

After passing through the barrier, which was located at the east end of the bridge, they turned north toward the border fence some thirty miles distant, driving past factories belching yellow smoke, and then vast pens of cows and pigs. Even with the windows closed, the odor seeped into the vehicle. At each site, there were lines of proles, their grubby, soot-stained faces impassive, bent to their work, seemingly unaware of the passage of the monitor vehicle.

Gravius had the driver stop the vehicle fifty yards from the sentry post guarding the heavy wrought iron gate. He and Leland-27 got out. Gravius thumbed the control that caused his visor to retract, his subordinate copied the movement.

The two men walked a few steps, and then Gravius held his hand out signaling a halt.

"You might be wondering why I intervened when the Chairman wanted you executed," he said.

"I . . . yes, citizen," Leland-27 said. "I thank you, but why *did* you do it?"

Gravius rubbed at his chin, regarding the young monitor with a serious expression.

"You might not understand . . . but, I'm your commander, and am therefore responsible for you. Besides, I saw that idiot . . . I mean, Citizen Robertson, tripped you causing the spill. I couldn't say anything about that, but I'll be damned if I was going to let you die for his clumsiness."

Leland-27 smiled.

"Thank you, Citizen Gravius. I owe you my life."

"Don't thank me yet, son. You'll still have to survive outside patrol duty for a good long while; at least until Citizen Cruz forgets the incident. And, by the way, if you ever repeat this conversation we're having to anyone, I'll kill you myself."

"What conversation?" Leland-27 said; a blank expression on his face.

Gravius-One smiled and patted his shoulder.

"Now, off with you, and keep your eyes open and your head down out there. The others have already been notified of your arrival."

Leland-27 saluted and lowered his visor. Turning he marched briskly to the gate to present himself to the duty sentry.

Gravius-One watched him go, a sad expression on his dark face.

# 5.

Three hours into their work detail in the pig enclosure, Hiroshi and Washington were covered in black muck and reeking of swine urine and feces, a dank, acrid odor that clung to skin and clothing and seemed to penetrate the very tissues of their nasal passages.

“Man,” Washington said. “You’d think you’d get used to it, but pig shit just smells worse the longer you have to breathe it.”

“You’re right about that.” Hiroshi nodded. “It’ll take hours washing the dirt off, and I don’t think they have soap strong enough to get the stink out. We’ll have to throw these clothes away.”

They were assigned to a team that included six other boys, all sixteen to eighteen years old. As the oldest, they were given the heaviest work, which consisted of shoveling the black sludge into large buckets and carrying it to a waiting wagon. The wagon would then go to a nearby agricultural complex where the manure would be spread as fertilizer for the crops, or to the power plant where it was used as fuel.

“I hope they don’t put any of this stuff on the potato crop,” Washington said.

“You know they put it on everything.”

“Aw, man; I’ll never eat another potato.”

“How will you know?” Hiroshi asked. “They mush everything up into that gray stuff they feed us. For all we know, they probably flavor it with pig shit.”

Washington made a face.

“Yeah, now that you mention it, the smell here does remind me of that stuff.”

They both laughed, which drew the attention of the black-clad monitor assigned to guard the work detail.

“All right, you two,” he growled. “Stop your talking and get to work.”

Hiroshi and Washington lowered their voices and bent their backs to moving the heavy, manure-laden containers, but continued to talk quietly.

“Dickhead,” Washington said under his

breath. “Standing around in his shiny black uniform like he’s something special.”

“Yeah, bet you he’s sweating like a stuck pig in that thing,” Hiroshi added.

“Sound of his voice, he seems to be about the same age as us.” Washington looked over at the monitor whose attention had been diverted by another prole who had dropped a bucket of manure, sending it splashing in all directions. “I wonder how he got stuck with keeping watch over pig dung.”

“Maybe he didn’t clean his dart gun.” Hiroshi nodded toward the wicked looking black flechette gun hanging on the monitor’s hip.

This caused another fit of laughing, which they tried to muffle by putting their hands over their mouths. Unfortunately, their hands were covered with the slick, black manure they’d been handling, which caused both to gag and spit. They found relatively grime-free sections of the sleeves of their singlesuits, with which they wiped their tongues.

“Yuck,” Washington said. “That does taste like the slop they feed us. I think I might just skip supper tonight.”

## 6.

Octavia Olympus sat at the tiny desk in the tiny cubicle that served as her office at Columbus Heights Crèche. The official indoctrination day was ended, and she was now engaged in the thing most in her profession detested; the paperwork. Assessment reports, student essays done in crabby, hard to read script, and dicta from her headquarters across the river.

She wanted nothing more than to burn every piece of paper and return to her small apartment on the other side of the river, to sit back with music playing on the sound system and a glass of wine in her hand. The only thing from this side of the river that she found interesting – besides the young prole, Hiroshi Jackson – was the fruit they grew in the fields, a portion of which was converted into flavorful wines, which she often imbibed after work to help erase the depressing scenes of the prole community from her mind.

But, of course, there was no way should could leave until she'd read and initialed all of the paperwork, so she pulled the first flimsy sheet off the tidy pile of documents and began reading.

The first dozen or so pages were assessment reports on the children under her care, with recommendations for further assignment; mostly to low-skill laboring jobs; and in one or two cases, recommendations for more advanced study to prepare the individual for one of the few technical jobs within the factories that had been reserved for proles. These were followed by a memorandum from the head of community orientation centers, the official name for the crèches, encouraging all supervisors to conserve power by turning off all lights and other electricity-drawing equipment from mid-morning to mid-afternoon as a means of alleviating brown-outs in the citizens' community areas.

It would mean a bit of discomfort for her and the rest of the attendants, but that was preferable to having electrical problems in her residence. It wasn't as if the prole children needed to get accustomed to having reliable electrical power. Once they left the crèche, they would be consigned to a small cubicle in one of the gray, crumbling high-rise buildings in the prole community, having to share bathing and toilet facilities with ten to fifteen other people. She had little sympathy for the proles, especially those left under her care five days per week. Hundreds of boring little minds that it was her job to fill with a love of community, meaning a love of laboring from dawn to dusk so that she and her fellow citizens could live comfortably.

Near the bottom of the pile was a paper that she saw only once a year, and one that often caused a cold feeling in her chest. A single sheet with a faint red border, it was the list of those in the crèche reaching the age of nineteen who had, for various reasons, been chosen for the annual culling. While she had little sympathy for the way her charges lived, what was left of basic human feelings inside her was repelled by the cold process of identifying those whose existence was considered of no utility to the community, and who would, therefore, have their existences terminated.

As usual, the names were alphabetized by surname, so she was near the middle of the page of thirty names before one leapt out at her:

## JACKSON, HIROSHI (NMI)

Her breath caught in her throat, and her heartbeat increased until she felt that she could hear the thumping.

While Octavia Olympus cared little for her students, there was one exception, and if asked to explain it she would have been at a loss. Young Hiroshi Jackson had first come to her attention more than eleven years earlier when he'd been brought to the crèche, when she'd been an attendant. He'd been screaming and resistant, kicking and biting at the monitors who brought him, and had refused to speak or respond to speech for the first week there, constantly asking for his mother and father. The monitor officer in charge of the detail that had brought him in had given her a brief summary of his history, and she found it fascinating.

Somehow, his parents had kept his existence a secret for seven years, hidden away in a subterranean chamber in the overgrowth near the great domed building with the strange woman's statue on top. His history was, fascinating enough for her, but the fact that at seven he could read, write, and understood math almost as well as she really caught her interest; that and his fierce independence.

She had watched Hiroshi grow from a

rambunctious little boy into a precocious adolescent, and finally into a quietly confident young man; self-assured, but still fiercely independent. She would not have called what she felt for him love; this emotion was not one that was discussed or acknowledged among citizens, and most especially not for a prole. She did not, in fact, understand the feeling. So, the hotness in her eyes, followed by the warmth of tears tracking across her cheeks after she'd seen his name came as a surprise to her.

The standard protocol when the list came out was to post it on the bulletin board at the entrance to the dining facility where the selected, along with everyone else, would be able to see it. It was, therefore, completely not in keeping with protocol when Octavia Olympus thumbed the call button on the communicator on her desk.

"Yes, headmaster," came the tinny voice of her assistant. "What can I do for you?"

"Find Hiroshi Jackson, and bring him to my office," she responded drily.

# 7.

Hiroshi, Washington, and Clementine had just finished supper and were heading to the roof of the building to gaze at the stars, or what few stars that could be seen through the perpetual odorous haze that hung over the community, when a stiff backed attendant stopped them in the hallway and informed Hiroshi that he was wanted in the headmaster's office.

Hiroshi looked curious, while his friends looked worried. It couldn't be good to be summoned by the headmaster after the end of the formal work day, when every one of the crèche residents was supposedly free to do whatever pleased him or her. The ever-present loudspeaker announcements continued – they didn't cease until a heartbeat before final lights out – but the proles who were confined to the crèches felt free to ignore them during the free period – or, blatantly ignore them, for they paid them little heed even during the day.

In his eleven years at the crèche, Hiroshi didn't remember ever hearing of anyone being summoned during rest period. This was the time when the attendants even disappeared. Oh, he knew they were still watching through the cameras they had mounted discretely throughout the facility, but during the free period, the stone-faced attendants went to wherever they went, leaving Hiroshi and his friends and fellow inmates to themselves.

As he walked the hallway from the dining facility to the administrative section, ignoring the puke green color of the walls, he wondered why he was being summoned. Olympus had already tried to embarrass him in front of the others for daydreaming in class; and he did it so much, he didn't think she would make a special issue of it. Maybe, he thought, the monitor at the pig enclosure had reported him and Washington for horsing around when they should have been working in bent-head silence. But, if that was it, he wondered, why wasn't Washington also being summoned?

His mind had considered and discarded several possibilities by the time he reached the door to the headmaster's outer office. The blank faced woman sitting at the desk in the outer office recognized him, and told him to have a seat until the headmaster was ready for him. Of course, he thought; ask me to hurry up and get here so I can wait until you're good and ready to tell me why you had me hurry here in the first place. He tried to keep his expression neutral as he sat on one of the hard plastic chairs lining the wall in front of the woman's desk. She thumbed a button on her desk communicator and mumbled something he couldn't clearly hear. There was a crackling sound of static, and she went back to staring at a paper on her desk.

Hiroshi lost track of time. His mind wandered. Back. Back to a time when he lived with his mother and father in the space beneath the city not far from the old building that his father said his grandfather worked in. He'd played in the tunnels forking off in all directions as a child, always careful never to go so far that he couldn't hear his mother's voice should she call him. But, he loved the times when his father would take him exploring, deep into the catacombs beneath what had once been, according to his father, the most powerful city on earth.

He really liked the special place. Deep, deep beneath the surface, out of reach of the black-suited monitors who kept track, or tried to keep track, of everyone in the prole community, was a large space that was filled from bottom to top with books. There were books of all kinds, in hundreds of languages; in precise type or ornate, unintelligible scripts, with pictures of strange people, strange buildings and costumes, and strange conveyances. The books opened up for him a world that had been destroyed before his birth, but remained alive within their pages – a world that he could only dream of.

Using some of the easier books in the English language, Hiroshi's father had taught him to read, write, and do simple arithmetic by the time he was four years old. By the age of six, he'd graduated to more advanced books, and in the process picked up a working knowledge of Spanish, German, French, and Italian. The non-alphabetic languages, like Chinese and Arabic remained a mystery to him. From a collection of atlases, he'd learned to read maps and had in his head an image of what the country, the world, had looked like before the ice caps melted, forever changing the shape of coastlines around the globe. He'd bombarded his father with a hundred questions, mostly about why, if there was land to the west of New Liberty, did people stay in what amounted to a crowded ghetto, with dirt, disease, and poverty.

After the men in black; the monitors; had found their hiding place and taken him away, never to see his parents again, he soon understood why.

The two of them had just returned to the cramped living space from the hidden cache of books. His mother was preparing supper on the little methane-powered hotplate, and the smells of the vegetables she was stir frying filled the space. Hiroshi had just turned seven, and was now allowed to help set the small table with the cracked china plates his father had found in the basement of a building a few miles away.

Hiroshi had just finished setting the plates on the table when there was a loud clatter, and the wooden door was turned to splinters with a loud bang.

His mother screamed, dropping the wok she'd been holding. His father rushed and grabbed Hiroshi, shielding him from the baton-wielding man in a black uniform, his face covered by a visor, who pushed through the door.

"Step away from the child, prole," the monitor said.

"Ulysses," Junko Jackson cried. "Don't let them take Hiroshi."

"What do you want?" Ulysses asked.

"You know what we want, prole. Now, for the last time, step away from the child."

"No, you can't have him."

"Ulysses Jackson," the monitor said in a dry, even voice. "You are in violation of New Liberty regulations concerning the education and housing of prole children. I am placing you and your mate under arrest, and the child will be transported to a crèche for proper indoctrination."

"No-o-o-o!" Junko shrieked.

Hiroshi was hugged close to his father's body, so he couldn't see what was happening, but he could hear. And, he heard the crunch of something hard contacting with something soft. He heard the moaning of his mother and father. Then, he felt himself being yanked from his father's arms. He began to scream.

As the monitor carried him up the ladder to the surface, he heard his father's muffled voice, "Always remember, Hiroshi. Don't ever forget. You are-" which was quickly cut off by the sound of a metal truncheon impacting with flesh, and a grunt of pain.

After that everything was a blur. He was still screaming when they took him from the monitor vehicle at the entrance to the Columbus Heights Crèche and turned him over to a bored looking attendant.

Yes, Hiroshi knew well why people stayed in New Liberty.

People stayed because they had no choice. New Liberty was surrounded by a twelve-foot-high wire fence topped with sharp razor wire. The fence was guarded around the clock by units of monitors armed with flechette guns, and anyone caught trying to get over, through, or under the fence was executed on the spot. New Liberty wasn't a ghetto; it was a prison, and the proles within its boundaries were prisoners – prisoners serving life terms of hard labor.

And now, Hiroshi felt, not like a student called to the principal's office, but a prisoner summoned by the warden to be punished for some infraction of the rules, written and unwritten, that controlled every moment of their lives. As he so often did when he thought about life in New Liberty, he felt anger welling up inside him. His face was hot and the muscles of his cheeks tight.

"You can go in now," the bored woman said.

Hiroshi didn't hear her at first, lost as he was in his thoughts, so she repeated it with a rising note of impatience.

He stood, brushing the wrinkles from the legs of his singlesuit, and walked to the door of the headmaster's office.

He pushed the door open and stepped through.

Hiroshi has seen many expressions on Octavia Olympus's face during his time in the crèche. The most common one was resigned exasperation at his antics, but on occasion he'd seen anger, and very rarely, something almost approaching a smile. What he saw now, though, was something he'd never seen before; Olympus looked sad. Her eyes glistened, and a muscle in her left cheek twitched constantly. She only briefly looked into his eyes, and then down at her hands which she held before her on the desk.

"You wanted to see me, headmaster?"

He stood in front of her desk, his hands clasped before him.

Finally, after what felt to Hiroshi like an eternity, she looked up. He had no doubt; there was sadness in her eyes.

"Have a seat, Hiroshi," she said.

That triggered an alarm bell in his brain. In all the years he'd been at the crèche, she had never addressed him by his first name. It was usually, *Mr. Jackson* in a tone of frustration.

He sat on the plastic chair she kept in front of her desk, his knees together, looking levelly across the desk at her.

"What is it? Why am I here?"

"You know, Hiroshi," she said. "While you can be supremely frustrating at times, you are one of the best students I've seen the entire time I've worked here in Columbus Heights."

There was his first name again; and, calling him a student. This wasn't good, and Hiroshi knew it, but, try as he might, he couldn't figure out what he'd done wrong.

"I'm sorry, headmaster," he said, and found that he really meant it. Old Olympus, despite her often sour expression, wasn't too bad. "It's just that the stuff you teach us is so boring."

Olympus sighed.

"If you think it's boring for you, think what it must be like for those of us who have to teach it year after year. But, we have no choice; we must teach the approved curriculum."

"But, you're only teaching us enough so we know how to turn machines on and off. I can learn that stuff in one day, so why do I have to listen to it for so many years?"

He knew the answer to his question. He remembered reading a book on brainwashing, and a novel, *Brave New World* by Aldous Huxley, shortly before the monitors invaded their home and took him away. He hadn't understood a lot of it until he'd been in the crèche for a few months, but he was a quick study, and it came to him. They were being conditioned; their minds indoctrinated, not just to labor incessantly and efficiently, but to *love* and *accept* it. They were being brainwashed, but he doubted that Olympus would admit such. And, she didn't, at least not directly.

"Our job is to make sure you leave here as productive members of the community," she said. "To do less wouldn't be fair to the community, or to you."

"But, if you taught us more, and we could choose what we do, wouldn't it be better for the community?"

Her expression went blank.

"The wisdom of the community is superior to the thoughts of the individual," she said in a mechanical voice.

*Holy cripes*, Hiroshi thought, *she's been brainwashed, too.* "I see, headmaster," he said. "But, it's still boring. I'll try to pay better attention in the future, though."

Olympus looked at him, blinking back tears.

"T-that's nice of you, Hiroshi. You know, I've always thought of you as the best student here; the one with the most potential."

"Uh, thank you," Hiroshi said. He began to hope that this might not be a case of him being in trouble. Maybe he was about to be told that he'd qualified for a technician job rather than being assigned as a mere factory laborer. On rare occasions particularly talented proles were sent to work as technicians under the supervision of a citizen technician. It was a small step above laborer, but even small steps were appreciated.

"But, I'm afraid . . . that is . . . I called you here tonight to deliver what won't be good news.

Hiroshi leaned forward in his chair, his eyes narrowed in concentration.

"I . . . oh, hell, there's no better way to do it," she said. She *never* used coarse language, even in front of the proles, and her indiscreet words caused her face to redden.

She pulled the single sheet from beneath the pile and pushed it across the desk at him. Her hands shook.

Hiroshi recognized the red-bordered paper. He picked it up and began reading the names, dreading what he knew he would find, and feeling a cold stab in his chest when he found it.

"B-but, why? I mean, if I'm such a good student, and I've never broken any laws, why would I be selected?"

She wiped at a droplet of liquid that welled from the corner of her right eye.

"I don't know, Hiroshi," she said. "I honestly don't know. I shouldn't even be telling you this. The normal procedure is for those chosen to be taken from class quietly after the first period. But, I felt I owed it to you."

Hiroshi breathed slowly and deeply, trying to collect his thoughts and calm his mind. His body felt cold and numb.

"Thank you, headmaster," he said quietly. "Will there be anything else. I'd like to be alone now if you don't mind."

Olympus stood and came around the desk. She rested her hand on his neck. He could feel the warmth of her flesh against his, and a slight trembling in her hand.

"I understand, Hiroshi. I mean, I don't really understand why this is happening, but I understand you wanting to be alone, I suppose. I wish there was something I could do."

He patted her hand gently, and stood.

"Thank you. I guess this is goodbye."

Taking a deep breath, he squared his

shoulders and walked out of her office. He felt like crying, but was damned if he'd let anyone see him do it.

When he was gone, Octavia Olympus sat behind her desk and wept quietly.

## 8.

Once outside the administration area, Hiroshi wandered aimlessly for several minutes, unmindful of his surroundings.

The feeling of cold fear that had greeted the news that he had been selected for culling was soon replaced with the heat of anger. His father's last words, 'always remember' kept replaying in his mind. He knew the meaning now, and knew what he must do.

He was torn between seeking Washington and Clementine out and telling them of his impending fate, but decided against it. They would be devastated enough, he knew, when the monitors came from him on the morrow. Instead, he decided to go to the place he often went when he wanted to be alone to think.

He made his way down the hall to the end, and through the door that led to the roof. Up the dark stairwell and out the door onto the gravel-covered flat roof, he found himself standing among a garden of cylindrical structures, pitted and red with rust. He walked to the edge, where he could look out over the Columbus Heights district of New Liberty's prole community. The only lights visible were the orange glows from the factory furnaces where the night shift labored away. The ever present smog from the factory's smoke stacks obscured the sky. Only the hazy oval of a full moon was visible through the yellow-gray pall of smoke.

Looking into the inky darkness, he imagined clearly what was not visible to his eyes; people crammed ten or more to a room designed for less than half that number, plumbing that spouted brown gunk when it worked, no electricity or ventilation, living in worse conditions than the animals destined for the abattoir. The thought made what he had to do easier; not easy by any stretch, but easier. There would, though, be no turning back. Once he was committed he would have to go all the way.

That thought caused sadness deep within his breast. His eyes burned with unshed tears. He'd been so absorbed in his thoughts, he hadn't been aware of Clementine's presence until he felt her slender arms slip around his waist.

"Why are you up here by yourself, Hiroshi?" she asked. She rested her face against his back. He could feel her warmth through his singlesuit.

He leaned back, and she hugged him closer. "I just felt like coming up here to look at the stars," he said.

"What are stars? I've never seen one."

No one in New Liberty had seen stars in the sky for decades because of the cloud of pollution that hung permanently over the community, but it was their standing joke.

"I can see them in my mind," he said. He'd also seen pictures of stars and constellations in the books his father had shown him. "They are beautiful."

"I wish I could," Clementine said wistfully.

"You know; out there beyond the boundary fence, there are no factories. I'll bet out there you can see the stars at night."

She laughed.

"Hiroshi, you have the wildest imagination. You know there's nothing outside the fence but wild animals and pollution so thick it would kill a person."

He turned to face her. Their faces were almost level.

"That's what they tell you," he said. "But, how do you know it's true?"

"They wouldn't lie. That comes from The Committee, and they represent the community. Anyway, why would they lie to us about something like that?"

He placed his hands on her shoulder, looking deeply into her eyes.

"That's easy," he said. "They tell you a lie like that so you won't want to leave, and you'll be happy to remain here as a slave. Think about it Clem, if there's so much pollution humans can't live out there, how could there be wild animals? And, why do they have gates in the fence, and guards outside? Tell me that?"

A look of confusion crossed her face. "I don't know. That's just the way things are. It's not for us to question the wisdom of The Committee."

He didn't want to be harsh with her, but on today of all days, despite the fact that she knew no better, having been raised on a diet of propaganda, it angered him that she was unable to use her brain to see the inconsistencies, in fact, outright lies they'd been fed.

"No, Clementine, that's what they *want* you to believe. Things are different, believe me."

"How do you know these things, Hiroshi? What makes you think you're smarter than The Committee?"

He'd been wanting for the longest time to share his secret with someone, with her especially. Now, with a sentence of death hanging over his head, it didn't make sense not to.

"Because, I've seen pictures of . . . the land . . . the world . . . on the other side of the fence. I've seen pictures of great cities where people lived in clean houses, and were able to choose their own work. I've seen maps of the land beyond the fence, and, Clementine, it's a big land, much bigger than you can ever imagine. It's a hell of a lot bigger than they tell us it is."

Her bright eyes were round as she gazed at him.

"Where did you see pictures and maps, Hiroshi? There are no such things, except the forbidden books which were all burned long ago."

"No, Clementine," he said. "They weren't *all* burned. Some of them were saved and hidden away where the monitors couldn't find them. I learned to read from some of them when I was just a kid."

"B-but, that can't be. Anyone caught with a forbidden book is culled."

"They are hidden in a place where no one can find them, but they *do* exist."

"Oh, Hiroshi, if they ever find out that you've been exposed to the forbidden books, they might send you for culling. You must never tell anyone else this."

He laughed harshly. "It wouldn't matter; doesn't matter anymore. They've selected me for culling anyway."

She stepped back, her face going pale.

"D-don't joke about things like that, Hiroshi." Then, her eyes went wide. "Y-you're not joking?"

"No; the headmaster showed me the list. That's why she called me to her office."

Clementine darted forward, burying her face in his chest, her body shaking.

"No, no, it can't be," she cried. "You're one of the best in our crèche. You should be selected to be a technician. Only the mentally deficient and criminals are culled. There must be some mistake."

He hugged her tightly, stroking her back. He could feel the front of his clothing becoming damp from her tears.

"But, they tell us that The Committee represents the will of the community, and the community is never wrong. If my being on the cull list is a mistake, then everything they've told us is a lie, right?"

She pulled back and looked into his eyes.

"I don't know. It doesn't make any sense. Oh, I'm so confused. What will we do?"

He grasped her shoulders, and leaned in until their faces were almost touching.

"Well, for one thing, I don't plan to be here in the morning when they come for me," he whispered. "Like I said, I've seen maps of the outside and wild animals or no, I think I'd rather take my chances with them than be turned into fertilizer for the potato fields."

"You're going to run away?"

"Yes, and, Clem, I'd like for you to come with me."

She pushed away from him. "Leave New Liberty? B-but, how would we live outside the community?"

"It's easier than you think. I've read books about living in the wild, and I remember most of what I've read. I know the plants and animals, and how to navigate."

Her oval face was streaked with tears. She

again buried her face against his chest.

"I d-don't know, Hiroshi," she murmured. "I love you, and I'd been hoping that when we left the crèche, we'd . . . you know . . . but, leaving the community. I just don't know."

"I love you too, Clementine, and I can't imagine living without you. But, I can't stay here and die like an animal. I don't want to leave you, but if I have to . . . I-"

She put a hand to his lips, silencing him. Then, her lips replaced her hand. Hiroshi felt a sensation that started in his chest and spread down, engulfing his whole body. As her warm, moist tongue pressed between his lips, and he tasted the saltiness of her, his breath caught in his throat. He was uncomfortably aware of the warmth of her body pressed against his, and the involuntary reaction it was causing. His mind was a maelstrom of emotions. He loved her with every fiber of his being, and even though he'd had no experience with members of the opposite sex, unlike many of the others his age in the crèche who often experimented in the darkened corners when the attendants weren't around, he'd read about, and remembered the physical and emotional processes involved. But, his feelings for Clementine went far beyond physical or even simple emotions. He loved her, and wanted to spend the rest of his life with her. The problem was, the community, in the form of The Committee, had decided that his life was of no use to the community, so it would be ended.

Had he not decided to run away, not wanting to die without ever having experienced physical love, he might have given in to his physical cravings, but he hadn't given up on being able to convince her to run away with him. Reluctantly, he pulled away from her, leaving her looking confused. Her breath was coming in ragged gasps.

"Hiroshi, what's the matter?" she asked. "Don't you want me?"

When he'd gotten his breathing under control, making clear speech possible, he kissed her lightly on the forehead.

"More than anything in the world," he said. "But, I don't want it to be like this. I want it to be . . . oh, I don't know . . . just not like this. Clementine, I love you, and I'd like to spend the rest of my life with you. But, in order to do that, we have to leave New Liberty."

Her lips quivered. Her body quivered. He felt the vibrations of her body through his clothing, and felt as if he would die. She looked up at him, her eyes wide.

"I-"

Her words were cut off by the sound of the door to the roof slamming against the wall as it was flung open. Hiroshi and Clementine started, and as they looked toward the door, stepped away from each other, their eyes wide in shock.

Two black-clad monitors stepped through the doorway and began walking toward them. With their visors down, in the reddish light cast from the glow of the factory furnaces glinting off the reflective surfaces, they looked like alien insects.

"Hiroshi Jackson," one of the insectoid forms said in a voice muffled somewhat by the visor. "You are to come with us."

# 9.

"No," Clementine cried, as she pushed herself between Hiroshi and the approaching monitors. "He's not supposed to go until tomorrow."

The two monitors, apparently expecting to find Hiroshi alone on the roof, stopped their advance. They looked carefully at the diminutive figure standing defiantly facing them.

"You are Clementine Adams," one said. "You are to step aside and return to your sleeping quarters. Hiroshi Jackson, you are to come with us."

The tone was mechanical, as if the man behind the mask was reciting something he'd memorized. It was also unwavering – there was no doubt he expected to be obeyed.

Hiroshi didn't want to go with the

monitors, but he also didn't want Clementine harmed. He took her gently by the shoulders and pushed her aside, moving forward.

"Okay, I'll go with you," he said.

*"Always remember."* His father's final words sounded clearly in his mind. Suddenly, he had an image of a book he'd enjoyed reading once he could make his way through the pages on his own. It was an English translation of Sun Tzu's *Art of War.* The passage that jumped out at him said roughly, *Use your enemy's strength to your advantage.*

He tried to look as non-threatening as possible as the monitor neared him. The second monitor lagged behind - which he was depending on. They had come expecting to face an unarmed prole teenager who would be intimidated by their uniforms and authority, thus they hadn't drawn their weapons. As the monitor withdrew a pair of plasticuffs from his belt, and reached for him, Hiroshi held out his hands.

Just as the monitor opened the cuffs to slip them around his wrist, Hiroshi grabbed his hand and pulled him forward. He'd already been moving forward, so the extra pull only caused him to speed up as he lost his balance. Hiroshi put all his strength into it and, turning to the side, flung the monitor at the brick wall that formed the ledge around the roof, causing him to crash face first into it. There was a crashing, tinkling sound as the visor cracked upon impact, followed by the crunch of the monitor's nose against the bricks.

Hiroshi immediately turned to face the remaining monitor, who was shocked into momentary immobility by what he'd seen. Hiroshi rushed toward him, and just before he reached him, leapt into the air, kicking his right leg out. He made contact with the man's breastbone, sending him staggering backwards.

The monitor back pedaled until he came into contact with the half-open door, and slid down to the floor. At this point, he began reaching for his flechette gun. Before Hiroshi could get to him, he had the weapon out and was pointing it at Hiroshi's chest.

Hiroshi halted, his breath caught in his throat as the monitor's arm stiffened. In the melee, he'd forgotten about Clementine. The *br-r-r-rp!* of a flechette gun from behind him caused him to jump. It also caused the monitor to jump as dozens of flechettes slammed into his body, causing it twitch like a marionette. Blood poured from the tears in his uniform, the dark fluid blending with the cloth. The monitor fell back, opening the door the rest of the way, as he slid down, he left a dark smear on the wood. His legs twitched and then he was still.

“Oh, shit,” Hiroshi said as he turned.

Clementine was holding the flechette gun in two hands, her eyes wide as she saw what it was capable of doing. Her body was shaking and her face was pale.

Just beyond her, Hiroshi saw the monitor he’d flung against the ledge, lying still in a bundle at the base of the brick hip wall, his head at an unnatural angle.

“Oh, shit,” he said again.

He gently removed the weapon from Clementine’s trembling hands.

“Is . . . he . . . dead?” she asked.

Hiroshi looked at the monitor by the door. His lifeless body was sitting in a widening pool of dark blood.

“Afraid so,” he said. “You got him good. Looks like the other one is dead as well. Where did you learn to shoot one of these things?”

“I saw one of the monitors do it once. He just pointed it and pressed that little thing hanging down. I couldn’t let him shoot you.”

“I owe you my life, Clem.”

He walked over and took the weapon from

her shaking hands, and kissed her on the forehead.

"W-what we do now, Hiroshi?" Her whole body had begun to shake.

"We have no choice, Clementine," he said. "Just hitting a monitor is a capital crime. We've *killed* two. They'll have no mercy. We have to leave."

She looked into his eyes. Her eyes were brimming with tears.

"Then, we shall leave, my love," she said simply. "We'll be together forever, right?"

"Forever," he said.

## 10.

Hector Cruz sat behind the large wooden desk that dominated his office. His expression was icy as he looked up at Gravius-One who was standing in front of the desk, his dark face impassive.

“You’re sure my orders will be carried out?” Cruz asked.

“Yes, citizen. I sent two men to the crèche. The prole boy will be brought to you tonight.”

“Very good.” Cruz nodded. “Make sure he’s not harmed . . . too much.”

Gravius nodded, turned on his heels and left.

Cruz pushed a call button on his desk communicator.

“Yes, citizen.”

"Citizen Halifax," Cruz said. "Good news; we'll know the location of the forbidden texts before this night is out."

"Are you sure?" Nigel Halifax asked. There was excitement in his voice. "This would give a great boost to our research."

"Oh, I'm sure. Ulysses Jackson knew where his father hid the texts that weren't burned. Unfortunately, an overzealous monitor killed him before I could interrogate him. I'm convinced, though, that he told *his* son the location, and now *he* will tell me."

And, once the brat had given him the information, he would join his father and mother – as fertilizer for one of the produce fields. Then he, Hector Cruz, would be the sole possessor of most of the world's knowledge. That, along with the life extending treatment Halifax was working on, would make him the most powerful person on earth. With the assistance of the militia when they returned to New Liberty he would begin to extend his rule until he *controlled* the world.

# 11.

At monitor headquarters, the duty officer was sitting at the front desk when Gravius walked in. The sergeant jumped to his feet.

“Commander, what are you doing here at this time of night?”

Gravius planted himself in front of the desk, glaring down at the hapless sergeant.

“Have your men acquired the prole Hiroshi Jackson as I ordered?” His voice boomed.

“I sent two men to get him as you ordered, citizen.”

“Should they not be back by now?”

Confusion distorted the officer’s face.

“Uh, yes, I suppose they should.” He thumbed the communicator panel on his desk, frowning. “They’re not answering. Should I send another unit to check on them?”

Gravius-One looked down at his subordinate. He took a deep breath.

“Do you think maybe you should?” His face contorted in an angry look. “Yes, you fool, you should check on them.”

The man scrambled from behind the desk and ran to a door in the back of the room.

“You two,” he yelled, pointing at two monitors who had been lounging on a bench. “Get over to the prole community, Columbus Heights Crèche, and see what’s keeping the two idiots I sent over there to pick up that prole kid. Don’t just sit there, move your asses!”

The two monitors jumped up and almost fell over each other getting out the door. The officer returned to the front office.

“I have two men on the way, citizen,” he said. “They should be reporting back within ten minutes.”

Gravius made a grunting noise and walked to the window. He stood there as immobile as a statue, looking out at the lights that illuminated the citizens’ sector of New Liberty. Taking a deep breath, he picked up a trace scent of the methane used in the factories and the power plant on the other side of the river, and immediately regretted it.

*"Being a citizen doesn't protect your sense of smell,"* he thought wryly. *"Burning shit stinks for citizen and prole alike."*

The duty officer, unaccustomed to the commander of the entire monitor force being in his office at night, and unnerved by the man's icy demeanor and the fact that he stood without seeming to even breathe, stood nervously in front of his desk. He'd wondered at the order to go into the prole community at night to arrest one young prole and bring him to The Committee headquarters; to the Chairman himself. It wasn't a tough assignment, taking an unarmed prole teenager into custody, so he'd sent two recently assigned rookies. Thinking about it now, though, standing there looking at his commander's unmoving form, they should have been back an hour ago. Columbus Heights was one of the near districts, and there wasn't any movement to delay them at this time of night. *"Shit, I should have checked on it before he arrived,"* he thought. *"If they've fucked this job up, I'll be lucky I don't get assigned to factory security in the northern part of New Liberty."*

While the officer was musing fretfully, Gravius-One was wondering why Cruz wanted this particular young prole. He clearly had something up his sleeve, and Gravius wanted to know what it was. The Chairman, never the most balanced personality, had been showing increasing signs of instability lately, he thought. That incident at the meeting when he'd insisted the monitor be executed, for instance. Punishment, yes; that was needed to maintain discipline and control; but, excessive and arbitrary punishment of another citizen, even a lowly monitor, was uncalled for. Now this. It was strange, and Gravius-One didn't like strange.

He decided that he would have the monitors bring the boy to him first. Maybe then he'd be able to determine why Cruz wanted him. Knowledge was power; in this case, the power to protect himself from whatever Cruz was planning, and his gut told him the Chairman was up to something that spelled no good for him or for others on The Committee – or for New Liberty for that matter.

His musings were interrupted by the beeping of the communicator on the duty officer's desk. The man bent over and muttered something into the mike. There was a response, but from across the room Gravius couldn't make it out. The officer, his face pale, stood and turned.

"What is the problem?" Gravius asked.

"The two monitors I sent to Columbus Heights are dead," the ashen-faced officer said. "And, the prole, Hiroshi Jackson, is missing."

*"The shit will hit the fan now,"* Gravius thought. "Find him," he ordered. "Find him, and bring him to me *alive.*"

# 12.

## *On New Liberty's western border and the Wilderness*

Hiroshi knew that it was only a matter of time before the two dead monitors on the roof would be discovered. When that happened, the monitors would raid every dwelling within a several mile radius of the crèche looking for him – and now, Clementine as well. His only advantage was that the two hadn't had a chance to use their communicators.

Taking the two flechette pistols and the spare clips from both, Hiroshi grabbed Clementine's hand and led her off the roof. Using a back hallway, he made his way out of the back of the building and across an adjacent vacant, weed-choked lot toward the west.

The lack of electric power in the prole community worked to their advantage. Most of the streets were in dark shadow. Using his memories of the city layout from the time before, and keeping to the shadows, they made it to within sight of the western fence before midnight. From a copse of trees on a low hill just east of the fence, Hiroshi lay, with Clementine at his side, for an hour, watching the monitors who guarded the interior, memorizing their patrol schedule and making note of their alertness; or lack thereof. He knew that the river was to their left, and that the fence crossed it at a point where it wasn't deep, but where the current was rapid. He noted that the patrols didn't go frequently to the river, spending most of their time checking the hills and forests to the area north of the river.

"What do we do now, Hiroshi?" Clementine asked quietly. "There are monitors everywhere."

He put his mouth close to her ear. "No; there aren't many of them to the south of here," he whispered. "We'll make our way to the river and cross the fence there. Once we do, we'll head west to the mountains."

She had recovered from the shock of the incident on the roof. Hiroshi knew that she now realized that there was no turning back. But, if they died, they would die free; and together.

"When do we go?" she asked.

He looked down the hill. The monitors had moved north, and he could no longer hear them crashing through the brush.

"Now," he said.

Crouching low, Hiroshi darted out of the trees with Clementine close on his heels. He ran down the hill until he was about twenty yards from the fence, and then turned south, keeping in the hip-high scrub as much as possible, and trying not to make too much noise.

It took thirty minutes for them to reach the river. Hiroshi knew they were near when the ground became wet and slippery and he could hear the roar of the rapids. The fence angled downward and disappeared into a stand of trees that lined the river. Hiroshi led Clementine into those trees. They stopped a few minutes to catch their breath. Looking back, Hiroshi saw no sign of the monitors. If they could make it to the river without being spotted, he felt there was a good chance they would make good their escape.

Clementine wiped at the wet leaves that clung to her clothing, and the droplets of water that coated her face and arms.

"Are we near the river?" she asked.

"Yes, very near," Hiroshi said. "Once we

catch our breath we'll move on.

He flicked at a leaf that was stuck to her shoulder.

"I have to warn you; in order to get to the other side of the fence, we'll have to go into the river."

He felt her body stiffen and heard a sharp gasp.

"Into the r-river? That's d-dangerous, isn't it?"

He wished he could have told her that it wasn't, but the truth was he didn't know, meaning that it was in all likelihood extremely dangerous. But, whatever dangers the river offered, they were unknown. If they didn't escape from New Liberty, he knew the danger they faced – instant execution by the first monitor they encountered. The monitors didn't take reaction against their authority lightly. Even being slow to move aside when ordered to by a monitor could earn a prole a severe beating, regardless of age or infirmity. He shuddered at the thought of how they would treat Clementine or him after they'd killed two of the dreaded security officials.

"No," he said. "It'll be cold, and being wet won't be too comfortable, but it's not dangerous." He crossed his fingers as he spoke and hoped that he wouldn't have reason to regret his lie.

As they drew closer to the river, even Clementine became aware of its presence. The mist in the air thickened. It was like walking through a gauzy curtain. And, the noise of the rapids was a continuous roar. When they broke through the foliage and stood on the banks, both mouths opened and their eyes went wide with awe.

This far out from the factory, the sky was less overcast, and a full moon cast a yellow glow over the landscape. Before them, the river was over fifty yards wide, with large rocks protruding above the frothy white water that rushed over and around them. They made their way gingerly down the slippery mud to the water's edge. It was slower at the sides, but only marginally. The fence was a few feet to their right, a black lattice work of wires on metal poles marching down the muddy bank and into the water, protruding six feet above the surface of the river until it rose up the far bank and disappeared into the trees.

Slipping and falling several times, they made their way to the fence. In the dim light of the moon, Hiroshi could see that Clementine's face and clothing was spattered with the black mud. Her eyes were like two shiny marbles peeking from behind a mask of dark clay as she looked at him. He looked down at himself, and saw that he, too, was covered with the slimy muck.

Hiroshi knelt at the fence, inspecting it where it went into the water. He could see that the wires were darker and pitted near the water, and knew that to be rust, the result of long exposure to the moisture. He reached down and tentatively touched the wire, noticing sharp barbs every two feet. Anyone trying to climb the fence would be torn and bloody before reaching the top, and then ripped to pieces by the razor wire at the top, if not by the flechettes of the monitors. He twisted the strand. It bent up from the mud, and snapped from its connection with the pole. He repeated the process until he'd pulled aside enough of the wire to enable them to squeeze through. Once on the other side, he pulled the strands back and pressed them against the pole. It wouldn't withstand close scrutiny, but might not be noticed by someone standing up on the bank.

He then took Clementine's hand and started north, staying near the water's edge. After nearly an hour of walking, they came to a place where the land rose sharply; a ledge that jutted out into the river; making it necessary for a choice between climbing up to the top of the ledge to pass, or going into the water. Hiroshi wasn't sure they'd gone far enough to be past the limits of the external patrol, so he was reluctant to climb up. On the other hand, for all of his reading, and being able to remember almost everything he'd ever read, reading about swimming and actually knowing how to do it were two different things. The river was shallow, but the current was swift, and the rocks on the river bed slippery. It was a difficult choice, but in the end, he decided to take a chance in the water.

He placed Clementine between him and the river bank and waded out to go around the ledge. At that point, the water was almost to their hips and he could feel the force of the current against his body, as if it was trying to push him over.

They'd almost made it past the ledge when Clementine's foot slipped on a rock and she fell backwards, her hand slipping from his. She shrieked and then was swallowed by the current.

Hiroshi had a moment of panic, and then he saw her head bob to the surface. She was being dragged out toward the center of the channel. He dove after her, sputtering as the water filled his mouth.

The combination of his flailing and the current carried him to her quickly. He grabbed her arm and pulled her to him, planting his feet in the silt, fighting against the current's effort to push them both down river. She sputtered, spitting up the water she'd swallowed when she went under, and squirmed in his arms.

"Don't worry, Clem, stay still," he said. "I have you."

He put his arm around her and, lowering his shoulder, fought the current to get them past the ledge. Once past the ledge, they climbed out of the water. They were both soaked through and shivering in the night air, which, despite the general rise in average temperature, felt chilly against their wet flesh.

Hiroshi remembered that a person whose body temperature got too low could suffer from hypothermia, and even die, even in the semi-tropical temperatures that prevailed. He had to get them somewhere that was dry and warm, or at least warm, or their journey would end with them dead on the muddy banks of the river.

Clementine's teeth were chattering so that Hiroshi could hear them by the time they'd climbed to the top of the river bank and made it to drier earth. There was still moisture in the air, so he kept moving north away from the river until they were out of range of the mist.

They entered a forest of oak, maple, black gum and beech trees, with a few fir and pine trees interspersed among them. The forest floor was a soft carpet of evergreen foliage and dead leaves. Looking up through the openings in the leaves, Hiroshi saw something he'd only before seen in books; an inky black star sprinkled with millions of pinpricks of flickering lights. He was seeing stars for the first time in his life. He took deep breath, and noticed something else. The air didn't contain the rank odor of burning methane or dried sweat. It was sweet with the scent of pine and honeysuckle, or at least these were the names he applied to the aromas assaulting his nose, based on the things he'd read. There was a soft sound, like gentle rain, as the breeze brushed the leaves and needles of the trees.

He pulled Clementine's shivering body close. "You smell that?" he asked.

"Y-yes, it's s-something s-sweet," she said. "I've n-never s-smelled anything l-like it b-before."

"Look up," he said.

She did, and drew in a breath.

"Oh, Hiroshi, it's b-beautiful. T-those are s-stars?"

"Yes, those are stars. Out here, you can see the sky, and you don't have to smell that stinky odor of burning shit all the time."

Of course, he thought, there's always the problem of finding food. Water was available in the river, but they'd need food soon if they were to keep moving far enough to be sure the monitors of New Liberty couldn't track them down. And, there was the issue of getting dry and warm. Clementine's shivering body against his reminded him of their most pressing need.

"Let's stop here," he said. "I'll make a shelter so we can get warm."

He eased her down against the base of a tree trunk, leaving her huddled there while he hollowed out a space between two large oak trees. He constructed a lean-to with dried branches and covered it with leaves and pine boughs. He then covered the ground underneath with a thick layer of pine needles.

He helped Clementine crawl in and then crawled in beside her, burrowing into the pine needles and pulling a layer over them, and then held her close. His teeth chattered so hard he was afraid he'd break them, and his body seemed as if it would never stop shaking. But, the pine needles soaked some of the moisture from their clothing, and their combined body heat and the foliage protected them from the wind. After a while, he didn't feel so cold, and the shaking eased. They clung desperately to each other. Hiroshi lay there, listening to Clementine's breathing and the sound of night birds and insects around them. At some point, he drifted off to sleep.

*"Tweet, tweet."* The sound yanked Hiroshi from a deep and dreamless sleep. The next thing he noticed was the warmth of Clementine, nestled in the crook of his arm, unaffected by the sound as she snored slightly. Then, he noticed the stiffness of his dried singlesuit, and the scratchiness as he stretched and slowly withdrew his arm from beneath her body. He could also feel the hardness of the flechette gun and clips that he'd put into his pockets.

He rolled slowly from beneath the makeshift shelter of twigs, branches and leaves, and rose achingly. As he took in deep breaths of the fresh, warm morning air, feeling it soothe his nostrils and throat, he became aware of the pressure on his bladder. He had to pee badly.

Looking down to make sure Clementine was still covered with pine straw and leaves, he then turned and walked into the brush downhill from where they'd slept. He undid the front of his singlesuit and relieved himself against a tree. With that pressure off, he began to notice the hollow feeling in his stomach. He was hungry, and he knew that Clementine would be famished when she awakened as well. He had to find food.

*"Tweet, tweet."* The sound came again from somewhere off to his left. He moved as quietly as he could through the bushes until he came to another clearing. Across the clearing he saw a bright red bird sitting on a small bush, alternating between eating the purplish-green berries it bore and singing. *"Must be calling its mate to inform him or her of the location of food,"* he thought, and that thought was immediately followed by the realization that if the bird could eat the berries, they were probably safe for him and Clementine to eat.

He hated depriving the bird of its morning meal, but figured that it would be able to find a new source. He rushed forward, causing the creature to *squawk* loudly and take off in a flurry of wings. He pulled one of the berries from the bush. It was small, not much bigger than his eyeball, and smooth to the touch. Tentatively, he took a small bite from it. The tart sweetness filled his mouth. It was the best thing he'd ever tasted in his life. Quickly, he ate the rest of it and picked a handful, cramming into his mouth, chewing and swallowing until the hollow feeling in his stomach was gone. He then picked more, shoving them into his pockets, and leaving dark stains on his hands and clothing. When his pockets could hold no more, he retraced his steps to where Clementine awaited him.

She was just beginning to wake up when

he knelt beside her, a handful of the berries held in front of her face.

Her eyes flickered open, unfocused at first, but when she was able to see clearly, she made a little *eep* sound and scurried away from him.

"That's okay," he said. "You don't have anything to be frightened of."

The sound of his voice seemed to comfort her. Her rapid breathing slowed.

"Whew! Sorry, but when I saw your face," she said. "By the way, you do know the bottom half of your face is all purple, right?"

"Huh! Oh, that must be from these." He held out the berries again. "You should try them, they're good."

She tentatively took one and put it in her mouth. After a few seconds, her eyes went all round and she smiled. "Hm, that tastes good," she said. "What are these?"

"I'm not sure," Hiroshi said. "I don't remember reading anything about them. But, I saw a bird eating them and figured they were safe for us to eat. I ate a lot and haven't felt bad at all."

He offered her the rest, but she shook her head.

“I . . . first, I have to . . . you know.” She made head motions toward the bushes.

“Oh, sorry,” he said. “I had to go too.” He pointed. “There’s a clearing over there. While you’re gone, I’ll build a fire. I saw some chestnuts, and I do know they can be roasted.”

She nodded shyly and eased out of the shelter.

Hiroshi busied himself clearing an irregular circle on the ground and erecting a small pile of dried leaves and twigs. He searched around until he found several small rocks, looking for the gray stones that he remembered reading contained pyrite or iron. He took two promising looking ones, about the size of his hand and struck them together sharply. He was rewarded with a tiny shower of sparks.

He knelt over the pile of leaves and twigs and shredded a few leaves, and then began striking the stones together over them. His hands were beginning to get sore and his arms tired before he was rewarded with a slight glow from the pile of torn leaves and a tiny wisp of smoke. He leaned over and blew gently until the red glow began to spread, and then burst in to flame, spreading quickly to the other leaves.

When the fire was wells started, he put

some larger pieces of wood on, waiting for them to ignite. The warmth from the small fire felt comforting in the slight chill of the morning air.

Satisfied that the fire was going well, he rose and walked north to a stand of oaks and chestnuts. He rooted around the base of the trees, filling his pockets with the nuts that had fallen, avoiding any that looked rotted or that had been picked at by birds or animals. Taking them back to the fire, he placed them in the edge of the flames. He found a green twig and used it to poke at the nuts, turning them so that all sides would get an equal amount of burning. He wasn't sure how long he should let them cook. His recollection of 'roasting chestnuts on an open fire,' was of the words of a song he'd seen in a book about ancient holidays, which unfortunately hadn't said how long the nuts were roasted, so he just let them stay in the fire until the outer husk started to burn, then, using the twig, raked them out.

By the time Clementine had finished her 'business,' Hiroshi had a small pile of the nuts on a large oak leaf, and the berries on another, placed on the ground near the fire.

"Wow, that smells good," she said as she sat down next to him.

"Dig in," he said. "While the nuts are still

hot."

They used their teeth to gnaw off the tough outer hulls of the nuts. The kernels had a strange, but nice taste. Clementine especially liked the berries, and by the time they'd finished eating, the bottom half of her face was as purple as Hiroshi's. They then went to the river and drank until Hiroshi felt his stomach would burst. They then washed the berry stains off their faces and hands, and returned to the shelter site.

Clementine's eyes widened as she tasted the roasted nuts. "Thmph besding ever eid," she said around a mouthful. Then, she swallowed. "That's the best tasting thing I've ever eaten. Why don't we have things like this in New Liberty?"

"I don't know. They're called chestnuts, and they grow wild out here."

"Those . . . what did you call them . . . berries? They were so-o-o good. I could eat them for every meal."

"We can," Hiroshi said. "And, lots of other things, too. You see, it's not so bad here as you thought."

"You're right, but what do we do now?" Clementine asked.

"Well, according to the maps I saw when I was small, the river goes north mostly, and then cuts west. We need to follow along it until we find a place where it's narrow and shallow enough to cross, or, if we're lucky, find one of the old bridges. Then we head south and up into the mountains."

Clementine's face was creased with worry as she looked into Hiroshi's eyes.

"But, Hiroshi, how will we live? You can find food, but where will we find shelter?"

"I built a shelter last night, didn't I? I found food this morning," he said. "When we're far enough away that we don't have to worry about the monitors, I'll build us a more permanent shelter. We have the monitors' weapons, so I can hunt. I remember books about hunting and growing food."

"So, the books are real? I heard people talking sometimes about them, but I always thought it was just stories. You've actually seen them?"

"Yes. My father used them to teach me to read. They're in a secret place that only he and I know . . . knew. I still remember everything I read in the books, and I know that what they've been telling us all this time is nothing but lies. Look around you, Clementine. The air is clean. You can see the stars at night. This is the way life was in the time before, not the way we lived in New Liberty."

Clementine took a deep breath. She looked up at the sky. It was deep blue and not obscured by a veil of yellow-gray smog. There were sounds around them; birds singing and the rustle of small animals moving through the trees.

"It is beautiful," she said.

After putting out the fire, they set out north, keeping the river to their left.

The trees and undergrowth grew thicker as they moved farther north, and the land rose slightly. At some places, they were in valleys surrounded on all sides by towering trees that clung to the slopes, at others they crossed vast undulating plains covered in chest-high grass. At one point, as the sun was high in the sky, they came out of a stand of trees onto a wide ledge with the hill rising on their right and a view out over a valley to the left, with the river a winding silver ribbon far below. The land to the right rolled gently out to the horizon, disappearing in a slight haze. Hiroshi had seen pictures of such scenes, but in the books, there had been houses and towns here and there. So far, except for a few rotting slabs of concrete that marked where there had once been highways, they saw no indication of human habitation.

From the ledge they made their way down until they reached the river again, at a point where it was only a few yards wide with massive rocks around which the water flowed. Stepping from one flat rock to another, they made their way across to the west bank.

As they turned southwest, the terrain became hillier, with less dense vegetation on the higher parts of the slopes. They now also saw more animals, including small animals like squirrels and raccoons, and larger deer and elk. The animals watched them warily as they passed, darting away if they came near. Clementine, who had never even seen pictures of such creatures, laughed and clapped her hands each time, sometimes running ahead of Hiroshi to see what was around the next turn.

"Don't run so far ahead," Hiroshi warned her. "Not all the animals out here will run from you."

"Oh, Hiroshi, don't be such a scaredy-cat. It's all so wondrous. I never knew there could be anything like this."

She was enjoying herself so much, he didn't want to discourage her, so when she darted ahead, he just picked up his pace to try and keep her in sight. At the same time, he was keeping his eye out for a place to stop for the night.

He was mentally reviewing what would be

needed in a camp site, including a properly secluded area for Clementine's toilet needs, so he lost sight of her for a moment. When he realized that she was out of view, he walked faster, so fast that, when he came around the bend in the trail, he crashed into her.

She was standing in the center of the trail, her body rigid, her arms stiffly at her side.

As Hiroshi looked past her, he saw what had brought her to a halt. He felt his heartbeat in his throat.

About fifty feet ahead of Clementine, standing in the center of the trail, was a black bear. It stood nearly six feet at the massive shoulders, making it six inches taller than Hiroshi. Its head was larger than his chest, and when it opened its mouth, Hiroshi saw teeth, one of which looked as thick as his wrist. The bear was standing on all fours, its massive claws dug into the gray earth. It swayed its head from side to side, and made snuffing noises as it looked at them.

Hiroshi placed his hands gently on Clementine's shoulders and pressed his body against her back. He could feel her trembling.

"W-what is that?" she whispered.

"It's a bear," he said.

"What do we do?"

Hiroshi did a quick search of his memory. He recalled reading that bears didn't normally attack humans unless they felt threatened or cornered, or the humans seemed to pose a threat to the bear's young. Since Apocalypse, though, with the greatly reduced human population, he doubted this animal had ever even encountered humans. The animal didn't seem to be preparing to charge them. In fact, it only seemed vaguely aware of their presence. Then he remembered that bears had bad eyesight, so if they made no sudden moves toward it, they might be safe.

"Back up slowly," he said quietly. "And, try not to make any noise."

Slowly, Hiroshi inched backwards, keeping his hands on Clementine's shoulders. She moved back with him, maintaining contact. The bear lifted its head and loudly sniffed the air. Hiroshi froze in place. He could hear the thumping of his heart, and his face felt cold.

Time seemed to stand still. The bear continued to bar the way ahead, although its attention seemed focused on something off to its left and up the hill where the trees grew thick and lush. Hiroshi tried to slow his breathing and put a damper in the quivers of fear to avoid spooking Clementine. He looked around to see if there were any trees nearby that they might be able to slowly move to and climb. He knew, though, that if they provoked a charge, they would never be able to outrun the bear. His only hope was to direct Clementine to a tree and hope that he would be able to distract the animal long enough for her to climb it. He did the odds of success in his mind, and wasn't satisfied with the outcomes.

A new emotion began to compete with fear – anger. It was just so unfair, he thought. They'd beaten the monitors, gotten past the fence and avoided detection by the monitors patrolling the border, and survived an encounter with the forbidden river, only to be eaten by a dumb bear. No, he chided himself; not eaten yet. *"Always remember."* His father's voice was a comforting presence in his mind. *"Where there is life, there's hope."* A quote from one of the books his father loved to read, the thick book with the pebbled binding and the gold-edged pages, that his father told him had been a book revered by many people.

Hiroshi spotted two beech trees with limbs about four feet from the earth. It would be easy for them to scale the trunk fairly rapidly, and the bear, which must, he thought, weigh several hundred pounds, wouldn't be able to go as high as they could. He began easing Clementine slowly to the right toward the trees.

They were almost off the trail when the bear suddenly wheeled left, and grunting loudly, dashed off into the trees. Hiroshi let his breath out slowly as the sound of the bear crashing through the brush came from farther and farther away.

"Is it gone?" Clementine asked.

Hiroshi turned and saw that she had her eyes clenched shut.

"Yes, it's gone. You can open your eyes now."

For the rest of their journey up the slope she stayed close to him, no longer interested in exploring their surroundings.

The sun was beginning to slide down toward the hilltops by the time the land leveled off. Ahead of them was a stand of trees, mostly evergreen, that Hiroshi thought would make a good camp site. Several yards past the tree line, he found a semi-circular clearing that rose slightly in the center. After building a small fire, he set Clementine to gathering pine cones from which he planned to extract the seeds, which were edible, while he gathered medium size branches and twigs to build a shelter. While he was searching for shelter material he found a small stream a bit downslope from their camp site, where they could get water.

They had eaten, gone to the stream to drink, and relieved themselves in a small clearing on the edge of the stream downstream from where they drank, and were sitting in the makeshift shelter watching the dying embers of their fire by the time the sun was down and the sky had turned a dark purple.

They sat for a while, gazing at the stars through the openings between the trees, a sight Clementine said she could never get enough of. When the fire was finally reduced to nothing but smoldering ash, they crawled into the shelter and burrowed beneath the pine straw with which Hiroshi had lined it, and were soon fast asleep.

Unlike the first night, Hiroshi dreamed. He dreamed of his parents, and the times they spent together, his mother mending his clothes and talking quietly with his father while he worked at writing or mathematics on a black slate they'd found in a pile of junk near where the books were hidden.

The sky was beginning to lighten when Hiroshi awakened. He wasn't sure what it was, but he had a sense of foreboding. It was quiet. He could only hear the sound of his and Clementine's breathing. And then, it struck him. It was *too* quiet. There should have been the sounds of insects and the birds that are up early seeking food, calling back and forth to each other. The quiet was unnatural, but nothing he'd read told him why it should be so.

Slowly, he eased out of the shelter, and, crouching, he turned in a circle, taking in his surroundings as far as he could see.

At first, he saw nothing. But, as he continued to look, little inconsistencies revealed themselves to him. Here, a bush moving slightly despite the lack of wind. There, a dark green shape that wasn't of nature.

Hiroshi stood and faced a large bush, behind which he'd seen one of the unnatural shapes.

"I see you there," he said. "Who are you, and what do you want?"

Suddenly, his breath caught in his throat. In front of him, several figures stood. They were men. Dressed in furs and assorted colors of cloth, they were armed with bows and spears. Some looked no older than him, but others looked ancient to his young eyes. Some were clean faced, but a few had various configurations of facial hair.

None of them were smiling.

A tall man, with a black beard that reached to his chest, and shaggy hair that was held in check by a brown band around his brow, stepped from the bushes. He fitted an arrow in his bow and aimed it at Hiroshi's chest.

"Who are you and what are you doing here?" the man asked in a deep, rumbling voice.

## 13.

The two older monitors were farther from the border fence than they'd ever been. And worse, they had a rookie with them who had *never* been outside before.

The monitor in charge was Hargrove-10. He was in the last week of his tour of duty outside the wire, and looking forward to going back to watching proles at a factory, or standing sentry duty outside the power plant. Out here, with the danger of a group of Wild Ones attacking you at any time, having to traipse around the booneys with an inexperienced man, he felt as if he had a large target painted on his back.

"Okay," he said. "I think we've gone far enough. Let's go back to the wire."

"But, the trail is leading toward the river," Leland-27 said. "Shouldn't we check it out? Maybe they fell in the river and drowned."

"If they fell in, they'd have washed up against the wire by now, idiot."

"Well, we should check that out, shouldn't we?"

Hargrove-10 sighed deeply. He turned to the third man, Alexander-12.

"How about this rookie, eh?" He laughed. "Can you believe him? He sounds like he's bucking for promotion to grade five or something."

"He stays out here, only thing he'll get is an arrow in his neck from one of the wild ones," Alexander-12 said. "I'm with you; let's go back."

"Hear that, rookie? Now, Alexander-12 here understands the chain of command. He knows that as a ten, when I say something, the thing to do is comply."

Leland-27 couldn't see the man's face behind the visor, but he knew he was smirking at him. He'd been the butt of every joke, and the target of every insult, some veiled, some direct, since Gravius-One had dropped him off at the gate. When the others learned that he'd been part of the elite guard at The Committee, the hazing only intensified. When the senior monitor on the gate was told that two proles had killed monitors and were probably going to try and get through the fence, Leland had been assigned with two monitors who had reputations as goof-offs to look for them.

They'd set out at first light, first going north along the fence, and after twenty miles without picking up a sign, had turned back south. They found the tracks along the bank of the river, and followed them along the river until they lost them in the forest.

They had been stumbling around in the trees for several hours, without knowing that they'd circled Hiroshi and Clementine's camp site three times. At that time, they'd been only a few hours behind the two fugitives.

"You're in charge," Leland-27 said. "But, the powers that be aren't going to be happy when we come back empty handed."

"Yeah, so what are they going to do, assign us to external patrol?"

Alexander-12 laughed. "External patrol, that's funny."

Leland-27 shrugged. The man had a point. Those in charge wouldn't be happy that they hadn't been able to find the fugitives, but they couldn't find what they couldn't find. The criminals were likely attacked and eaten by wild animals anyway, and if not that, the wild ones would kill them – or so every man on external patrol believed.

That none of them had ever *seen* a wild one was completely irrelevant; they believed in them. It was also a good excuse for limiting the range of their patrols.

"I suppose you have a point," he said. "Shit, let's get back to base. The bugs out here are driving me crazy."

# 14.

Hiroshi froze in place, staring at the apparition before him. Like everyone else in New Liberty, he'd heard stories of the wild ones, the people who lived in the forest and refused to join the community, but until now had thought it a mere tale to frighten people and dissuade them from trying to escape. Now, he knew them to be real, and from the sharp looking points of the arrows that were all aimed at him and Clementine, just as dangerous and deadly as the stories said. Along with the weapons, their dress added to their imposing appearance. Many were wearing jackets made from what looked like the pelts of animals, while others wore multicolored shirts over tan or blue pants. Except for a couple who looked not much older than Hiroshi, all had facial hair, ranging from thin mustaches to bushy beards. They looked to Hiroshi like the pictures he remembered of ancient barbarian warriors like the Gauls or Huns.

"I asked you a question. Who are you, and where are you coming from?" the bearded man demanded.

The circle of men had tightened. Clementine huddled against Hiroshi, her eyes wide with fright, and her body quivering like leaves in the wind.

"I – I am Hiroshi Jackson," he said. "This is Clementine Adams. We came from New Liberty."

There was a general murmuring from the men. Some brandished their weapons menacingly.

"I say we kill 'em and be done with it," a skinny man with a wispy mustache said.

The bearded man waved the group to silence.

"That's not the way of Freelanders," he said. "No one can be deprived of life without a chance to defend or explain themselves." He turned back to Hiroshi. "So, Hiroshi Jackson, you're from New Liberty, is it? How is it the two of you come to be way out here?"

The story poured out. Hiroshi told of being informed that he'd been selected for culling, and how the monitors had come for him on the roof of the crèche. There was more murmuring when he described slaying the monitors and the wild journey he and Clementine had taken.

"Abraham, you ain't believin' that story, are you?" the skinny man said. "I bet these two are monitors sent out to infiltrate us."

The bearded man shook his head.

"I have to admit, Reuben," he said. "You make a good point. I've never heard of any of the slaves of New Liberty fighting back against the monitors and their weapons."

"But, we did," Clementine said. "Hiroshi broke one's neck, and I shot the other one with the gun I took from the one he killed. He was about to shoot Hiroshi, and I couldn't let him do that."

This brought laughter from most of the group. Had he not been so frightened, Hiroshi would have laughed himself. Tiny little Clementine, hands on hips, staring up at this intimidating looking group of armed men and describing how she'd killed someone threatening Hiroshi – describing it with such passion – *was* an amusing sight.

"You're quite the hellion, little girl," the bearded man said. "I'd hate to get on the wrong side of you."

The men laughed more. But, the wicked

points of their arrows remained steady.

Hiroshi decided to take a big chance, knowing their lives depended on convincing this band of rough looking men that they were no threat.

"We brought their guns with us," he said. "We have them in our pockets. You can have them."

He raised his hands to his shoulders, nodding at Clementine to do the same.

The bearded man lowered his bow and approached slowly. He patted Hiroshi's side, feeling the flechette gun in his pocket. Gingerly, he withdrew it and put it in his belt, and then repeated the process with Clementine. Hiroshi slowly lowered his hands and removed the spare clips, first from his pockets and then from Clementine's, and offered them to the bearded man, who took them and put them into a pocket of the tan colored pants he wore.

"You're either telling the truth," he said to Hiroshi. "Or, you're pretty clever. You want to tell me how two unarmed kids defeated two armed monitors?"

"When they came for me, they didn't think I would cause any trouble," Hiroshi said. "They didn't even draw their weapons. I think they thought I would just meekly go with them. I remembered reading in a book about using the strength of your opponent against him." There was a collective gasp from the men who now surrounded him.

"You can read?" the man, Reuben asked.

"Yes," Hiroshi said. "My father taught me."

"You have to come up with a better story than that, son," the bearded man said. "I happen to know that children in New Liberty are taken from their parents when they're born, and the only books allowed are instruction manuals."

"That's true, but my father knew where many books were hidden. He showed me, and taught me to read from them when I was small."

"And, Hiroshi wasn't brought to the crèche until he was seven," Clementine added.

The bearded man's eyes narrowed.

"Your folks kept you hidden for seven years?"

"Yes," Hiroshi said. "But, one day the monitors found our home, and they took me away."

"What happened to your parents?"

"I don't know." Hiroshi felt the hot sting of

unshed tears as he thought of his mother and father. "But, I think the monitors killed them."

"Did they find the hidden books?"

"No. I don't think the monitors thought to ask. If they'd found them, there would have been a public burning."

"There would have been at that." The man rubbed at his beard. "Okay, we'll take you two to our settlement. There's someone there who can verify what you're saying."

"You sure that's a good idea, Abraham?" Reuben asked.

"If the boy's telling the truth, we have to know. We need to take him to Rebecca."

# 15.

The men set out to the south, with five out in front and the rest following behind. The bearded man, who introduced himself as Abraham Moses, one of the leaders of the Freelanders, walked in the center of the group with Hiroshi and Clementine. He'd put his bow across his shoulder, but those behind them kept their weapons at the ready.

They walked in silence for an hour. Hiroshi was brimming over with curiosity, but Moses's stern expression made him reluctant to ask questions. Clementine, on the other hand, wasn't as sensitive to the man's moods.

"Where are we going?" she asked.

Moses frowned down at her.

"Just full of questions, aren't you, missy?"

"I just want to know is all," she said innocently.

He laughed.

"Okay, guess you got a right to know," he said. "We call it Freeland."

"I thought that was the name of your country," Hiroshi said.

"Country? We got no country, boy. We just got one little settlement of about five thousand people, and we call it Freeland."

"You only have five thousand people? But, they act so afraid of you in New Liberty. They have monitors patrolling the borders because they're afraid you'll invade. There are more people working in one of our factories than you have in your whole country."

"Hell, boy, it's not the numbers they're afraid of," Moses said. "It's the idea of people thinking for themselves that scares your New Liberty leaders. They got you people under their control, and they're afraid we might infect you with free will."

"Huh?"

"I reckon you're still too young to understand. You will, though, that is, if you're who I think you are."

Hiroshi asked who Moses thought he was, but the man refused to be drawn out further. Instead, he launched into a history of Freeland.

"Most of the people living in Freeland now were born there," he said. "We probably only have a couple hundred people, like me and Rebecca, who came from other places." When Hiroshi gave him a wide-eyed look, he laughed. "I know I don't look it, boy, but I'm seventy years old. I used to live in a place called Baltimore. But, when things started going bad, and the sea levels rose, wiping out most of the coast, me and my family moved out to West Virginia.

Moses looked around as they walked. He waved a hand, taking in their surroundings.

"Out here it was tough at first. I mean, we were a bunch of city folks. But, people looked out for each other. Not like it was back in the cities, where it was dog eat dog. Then, the preachers and the politicians got in bed with the militia and took over the cities, and things got worse. New Liberty's not the only one, you know. They got another one west of here, what used to be Cleveland, Ohio, which is just as bad as New Liberty. They call themselves Independence. We steer clear of both places, but for some reason, the people in New Liberty seem to be a bit more paranoid about us than the leaders over at Independence."

"They wanted to kill Hiroshi," Clementine said. "They're really evil people."

"They didn't start out that way," Moses said. "You have to understand; things were pretty bad when the world started to fall apart. People kind of went crazy. At first, the politicians just tried to restore order and stability. It was so bad, though, they had to use some pretty heavy handed methods to do it. It worked, too. When the militias started enforcing the rules with summary executions, peoples' taste for violence evaporated."

"But, they're still killing people," Hiroshi said.

Moses nodded, pulling at his beard again.

"Well see, that's the problem with people who have power. It corrupts them something fierce. The more they have, the more they want, and the worse they get."

"How do you avoid it in Freeland?" Hiroshi asked.

"In Freeland, no one has *power*," Moses said. "What we have is responsibility. They call me the leader, for instance. But, that's only because I'm old and experienced. Most things I do, I have to get the okay of the

Council of Elders. If they disapprove something, that's it. In addition, I share the leadership with my wife, who has also been in the community a long time. She was a teacher before things went bad. Worked at a school in Richmond, Virginia, until they burned it down and ran off the teachers. She made her way out here about a year after I did. Ran our schools for a while, and then the two of us married, and well, the rest is a story for another time."

"We have The Committee," Clementine said. "But, they still treat us badly."

"How many- what do you call yourselves – oh yeah, proles; how many proles sit on this committee of yours?"

"Only citizens can be on The Committee," she responded.

"In Freeland, anyone can be elected to the Council of Elders after they reach the age of eighteen, and the members have to stand for re-election every two years. That way, no one gets drunk with power. When you know you have to keep the people happy, it tends to curb the instinct to lord it over them. In Freeland, it's not the leaders who are the boss, it's the people."

"I read in a book that the U.S.A. was like that," Hiroshi said.

“What’s the U.S.A.?” Clementine asked.

“That’s what this country used to be called. That’s short for United States of America,” Moses said. “They say it stretched three thousand miles east to west from one ocean to the other, and nearly a thousand miles north to south.”

“They elected the leaders just like you say you do in Freeland,” Hiroshi added. “I wonder what went wrong.”

“A whole bunch of things,” Moses said, shaking his head. “Some were caused by nature, but a lot were caused by just plain greed and stupidity. When things started falling apart, books were burned and schools were closed, leaving people pretty much to their instincts in order to survive. When people like your committee took charge in the cities that were left, they instituted strict controls in their efforts to restore some semblance of order. That led to dictatorships in at least the two we know of.”

“How did you avoid it in Freeland?”

“People who came out here did it to get away from the disorder at first. When we realized that we had to join together in order to survive, we tried to rebuild what had been lost. We were fortunate that a lot of the people who came here had been teachers and intellectuals fleeing the persecution that was developing in the cities. They remembered things like individual freedom and respect for human rights. The rest just sort of grew out of that initial impulse."

Hiroshi found the man's story fascinating. So much so, in fact, that he'd lost track of time or how far they'd walked. He was surprised, therefore, when they entered a large clearing in the forest and Abraham Moses called a halt.

The men who had been in front of the group had already made a fire and placed logs around it for seating. Someone had killed a deer, and one of the men was skinning and gutting it. Clementine made gagging noises when she saw the man pull a mass of bloody guts from the animal's carcass.

"Looks like we eat well tonight," Moses said.

"Eew! What is that?" Clementine asked.

"That, little girl is a deer, and when it's cooked it'll be venison. Best meat the woods have to offer."

"Y-you *eat* that?"

"Don't you get meat in New Liberty?"

Hiroshi laughed. "Maybe, but since everything's all mushed together into a tasteless gray paste, there's no way to know for sure."

"Well, you're in for a treat tonight," Moses said.

The men hefted the deer's carcass, slipped a long green sapling through from the throat and out the rectum, and then placed it on two tripod saplings at either side of the fire. Very quickly, the smell of the roasting meat filled the air in the clearing. Hiroshi found himself remembering his mother cooking, and the smells that came from the pot. His mouth began to water in anticipation. Even Clementine sniffed appreciatively.

"It does smell good," she said.

And later, when the meat was golden brown all over and some wild roots the men had gathered had been roasted as well, they sat around and the cook sliced off generous chunks for everyone. Hiroshi immediately bit into the meat, juice running over his chin. Clementine was more tentative at first, nibbling at the crusty meat, but when it hit her tongue, her face lit up with a smile. She quickly devoured the first piece, and looked around for another, which quickly came. She looked at Hiroshi with a mischievous glint in her eyes.

"This is a lot better even than your chestnuts," she said, wiping daintily at the line of grease that ran down over her chin.

Two toilet areas were set up downhill from the camp site, one for the men, and a smaller one set off for privacy for Clementine. As darkness fell, with their stomachs full, Hiroshi and Clementine settled down on a bed of leaves and straw and fell into deep, satiated slumber with their arms wrapped around each other.

They were awakened the next morning by the sound of the men stirring in preparation for the day's march.

"Rise and shine, you lazy bones," Moses said. "We'll be reaching the settlement by midday, but we need to get started now."

After a quick breakfast of venison left over from the previous evening's repast, they set out. Clementine found the cold meat not quite as good as it had been hot and fresh off the fire, but still delicious. To Hiroshi, the cold meat actually tasted better. He remembered reading about how the original settlers in the area, the Amerinds, would smoke strips of deer meat and dry it, and then keep it with them to eat while they were on the trail or hunting. He made a mental note to talk to Moses about that. It would enable the Freelanders to spend longer times on patrol without having to stop to hunt. He shook himself – he was already thinking of himself as a Freelander, and he and Clementine hadn't even been formally accepted into the community. *"One step at a time, Hiroshi Jackson,"* he chided himself. *"One step at a time."*

The forest through which they traveled seemed to go on forever. Around mid-morning, the ground started sloping upwards slightly and the trees thinned out. Then, they came to a place where steep cliffs rose up to either side of them. Warped shrubs grew up between the rocks that lined the cliff walls. The path between the walls was narrow, only wide enough for two people to walk abreast.

The cliff walls were so high Hiroshi could only see a dark blue sliver of sky over their heads. Walking in such a tight space, it was hard to talk, so they walked in silence.

When they'd walked for what seemed like forever, Abraham Moses, who had been walking just in front of them, raised his hand signaling a halt. The two men he'd sent ahead were standing in the trail waiting for him. Those who followed closed up.

"Why are we stopping?" Hiroshi asked.

Moses pointed ahead.

"Trail drops down into a valley just up ahead," he said. "We have a sentry post. To make sure there are no surprises, when we come back, we enter in a tight group so the sentry can get a head count. Since we're two more with you two, it's important we stay together. Okay, let's move up."

Without warning, a broad-shouldered man brandishing a spear stepped into the path, blocking their way.

"Welcome back, Abraham," he said in a booming voice. "Who that you got with you?"

"Couple of strays from that hell hole New Liberty," Moses said. "They run away from home."

"Well, y'all go on through. They'll be serving up lunch pretty soon."

"Will there be more venison?" Clementine asked.

Moses, Hiroshi and the other men laughed. Clementine looked puzzled.

"Welcome to Freeland," Moses said.

# 16.

Hector Cruz was furious.

He was more than furious, he was apoplectic. His face was red, his eyes were red, and he sputtered when he wasn't choking on his on phlegm.

"What do you mean they got away?" He roared. "I want the monitors who let them escape executed immediately."

Gravius-One looked across the round table at the Chairman. His dark face felt hot and his stomach bubbled with barely suppressed anger.

"That won't be necessary, citizen," he said. "The proles killed them before they escaped."

Cruz looked at the monitor commander with his mouth agape. His lips quivered.

"What kind of people do you have in your

organization, citizen?" he asked when he'd regained his composure to a degree. "Two armed monitors can't arrest one eighteen-year-old prole?"

"The officer in charge of the station sent two new men." Gravius didn't really fault the man, but an example would have to be made. "They made the fatal assumption that the prole would be intimidated. He wasn't, and moreover, he was not alone. The two proles attacked and killed them. The officer who sent them will be severely disciplined."

"The prole Hiroshi Jackson has to be caught and brought to me." Cruz pointed a finger at Gravius.

"That, I'm afraid, is impossible, citizen. The two proles made it through the fence. I had men searching for them as far as the place where the river turns north, but their trail disappeared. If they haven't been killed by wild animals, the Wild Ones will have killed them."

Cruz slapped a hand against the dark wood of the table top, causing Gravius, who was not given to being easily startled, to flinch in his chair.

"I don't want excuses, Citizen Gravius, I want results. I want that prole, and even if it means entering the Wild Ones' territory, you *will* find him and bring him to me. He's not dead. I would know if he was dead." He uttered the words with such cold determination Gravius felt a hollow sensation in his chest.

*"He's gone completely insane,"* he thought. *"And, that makes him even more dangerous than usual."* He stood, his hands at his side, looking down at Cruz, and making an effort to keep the fear he felt from showing. "Very well, citizen," he said. "I'll send another search party out."

He inclined his head a fraction of an inch, just enough so as not to seem insubordinate. Cruz waved a hand as if he was brushing at an annoying insect, dismissing the monitor commander without a word.

# 17.

## *Freeland*

As they came over the hill, Hiroshi looked down at the valley spread out before them. Freeland wasn't at all what he'd expected.

Surrounded on all sides by medium high, mountains with rounded tops, the valley was wide, but even longer, stretching into the distant haze. Hundreds of buildings of all sizes, with streets and paths in a neat grid, was a few hundred yards from where the path downslope from where they stood. Well-tended fields covered the rest of the valley. As they came off the slope onto the path, which Hiroshi could see now was beaten earth, he noticed the variety of people in Freeland. Children ran and played among the houses, which were mostly made of rough-hewn logs and roofed with shingles made of slabs of bark. Elderly people sat on chairs or logs near the houses, watching those children who were too young to frolic, sewing, or just gazing at the sky. Hiroshi had never seen people who were not engaged in some form of productive activity. He had, in fact, never seen people of such advance age before.

In the few fields they passed, he noted that both men and women worked side by side. They wore various clothing, not the drab singlesuits he was accustomed to. But, what struck him was the absence of monitors ensuring that the work was done.

“Why are the workers scattered about so?” he asked. “Wouldn’t it be more efficient if they worked together?”

“Oh, they do get together when there’s a big job,” Moses said. “Like harvest time in the grain fields, or when a barn or corral has to be built. But, for the rest of the time they work their own property.”

Hiroshi stopped so suddenly, Clementine bumped into him.

“People here own property?” he asked.

“Of course,” Moses said. Then his eyebrows lifted. “Oh, I forgot. They abolished private property in New Liberty long before you were born. You know, we tried communal property here in Freeland at the start, but it didn’t work. When everyone owns a thing, no one assumes responsibility for it. We found that when people have some sense of ownership, they work harder and produce more."

Clementine looked around at the workers in the field nearest them. She put her hands on her hips.

"This seems awful inefficient," she said. "If no one is making central decisions on the work to be done, how do you make sure enough of what you need is produced?"

"Oh, people figure it out, young lady. The farmers grow crops based on the previous year's demands, usually producing a bit more as a cushion, bakers bake enough bread to satisfy current demand, tailors make clothing from orders from customers, and so on. It's not one hundred percent efficient, but then again, people aren't machines. One other advantage we have is that with the average temperatures above what they were in the past, we can grow crops year round."

She shook her head, not really comprehending what Moses was saying. It was all so strange. It was strange to Hiroshi too, but he had at least read about such economic systems in some of the hidden books. It had been called market capitalism, a system where production of goods and services was based upon demands from consumers. In the United States, that system had replaced a more feudal economy based upon indentured servitude and slavery. In New Liberty, that system had been brought back with a vengeance.

They continued to walk through the settlement, passing an open air market where people bartered all manner of goods and services, while children darted in and out among the stalls or piles of merchandise, another sight neither Hiroshi nor Clementine had ever seen.

Moses stopped in front of a small cabin. He rapped lightly on the door. After a few moments, the door swung inward and a small figure emerged from the gloomy interior.

"Good day, Abraham," the woman said. "You're back, and I see you brought company."

She was small, not much taller than Hiroshi, and even smaller in build. Her hair was snow white and cropped close to her round skull. Her face, with broad forehead and high cheekbones, was so dark the shadows were almost blue. Her almond shaped eyes were light brown, almost yellow, and bright with amusement as she looked at Hiroshi and Clementine.

"Yes, Rebecca, these two youngsters

escaped from New Liberty. We found them in the forest on the other side of the mountain. The lad is Hiroshi and the girl is Clementine. This fine lady is Rebecca Stennis, and I believe she might just be the oldest resident of Freeland."

The old lady laughed and slapped Moses on the forearm.

"You mind your manners, Abraham Moses. I might be old, but I can still whip your behind. Come on in, all of you. I just brewed a pot of dandelion tea, and I hate drinking alone."

She stepped aside to let them enter. The room they entered was lit by the light of a single candle set in a holder on a table in the center casting a warm glow over everything. Next to the candle was a shiny metal pot with a curved spout and handle, beside which sat six metal cups. The room was sparsely furnished but neat, much like the woman who occupied it.

As the three took seats around the table, Rebecca Stennis returned to the small settee where she had been sitting and began pouring the steaming tea into cups. All the while, she eyed Hiroshi.

"Tell me, young man," she said. "What is your family name?"

Huh?" he asked. "Oh, you mean the name of my father? His name was Ulysses Jackson. My mother's name was Junko."

Her eyes narrowed and she nodded.

"Do you know the name of your grandfather? Your father's father?"

"Uh, I believe it was Ban-, no, it was Benjamin."

Her eyes flew wide and she reached across the table to grasp Hiroshi's hands.

"Yes, I can see it now," she said. "You have his eyes."

"You . . . you knew my grandfather?"

Oh yes, I did. The three of us, him, his wife, and me, worked at the Library of Congress. That was a government building in which copies of almost every book, newspaper, magazine, or pamphlet that had ever been published was kept. You could say it held the world's knowledge. When the book burnings started, we were assigned to move selected books to a safe place. We worked night and day on that. Near the end, when we knew they were coming to sack our building, your grandfather tried to get his wife and me to leave for safety. She refused, but the two of them insisted I leave. I got out of the building just ahead of the mob. I never found out what happened to them, or to your father, who was just a child at the time."

Hiroshi told her what his father, Ulysses, had told him. This brought tears to her eyes. Her expression turned to anger when he told her what had happened to his father and mother.

"I guess that means they found the hidden books," she said.

"No," Hiroshi said. "I don't think so. I was young when the monitors came, but I remember my father not telling them anything, and I remember the last thing he said just before they took me away. He said 'always remember.' I didn't understand it at the time."

"But, you do now, don't you?"

An image came into Hiroshi's mind, a long, winding underground passage, lined with rusty pipes and frayed wires, leading to a thick iron door. The door was rust encrusted and looked as if it was welded permanently in place. But, this was deceptive. If pressed in just the right place, the door swung inward smoothly. Behind was a large room, that had originally been lit by fluorescent fixtures set in the high vaulted ceiling, but when the electricity finally failed, by candles and then torches set in sconces on the walls. The floor was covered in gleaming white ceramic tiles. Hiroshi remembered his shoes making clicking sounds as he followed his father between the towering stacks of books that were arrayed row upon row from one end of the room to the other end in the far distance. There were books of all kinds, large and small, thick and thin, some bound in hard cardboard, some in paper, and some in leather and other elegant looking materials. But, it was what lay between the covers that most fascinated him. Whether words or pictures, once he learned to read, he spent many an hour in the room, lying on his stomach under one of the torches flipping the pages and being transported to a world beyond his imagining.

"Yes," Hiroshi said. "He meant that I should always remember what I read. He also meant that I should remember where the books are kept, and I do."

The old woman's eyes glistened as she blinked back tears. She gently caressed Hiroshi's cheeks and looked up at Abraham Moses.

"He is the one, Abraham," she said. "He has finally come."

# 18.

"What did she mean, I'm the one?" Hiroshi asked.

Abraham Moses had made their excuses and said goodbye to Rebecca Stennis, stating that she needed to rest. She'd complained until he promised that he would bring Hiroshi back after he'd gotten him and Clementine settled.

The three of them were now sitting in the modest cabin that Moses shared with his wife Sarah. She had brewed a pot of tea and was pouring cups for each of them.

"That's a long, and pretty complicated story, son," Moses said.

"I have nothing but time," Hiroshi said.

Moses laughed, and slapped his knee.

"The boy has a right to know," Sarah

Moses, a tall, broad-hipped woman with brown hair flecked with gray pulled back tight against her skull, and smiling gray eyes, massaged her husband's shoulders. "You know it."

A look passed between husband and wife. Hiroshi noticed it. He leaned forward, fixing Abraham Moses with a steely gaze.

"You're right as usual." Moses sighed. "Okay, boy, sit back and I'll tell you what I know.

Clementine perched on the arm of Hiroshi's chair, her hand on his neck protectively.

"I guess I have to start with when Rebecca first came here," Moses continued. "It was right after we started building the first houses. She came stumbling off the mountain, more dead than alive. She'd walked all the way from Washington – New Liberty was still known as Washington, DC at that time. We took her in and tended to her until she recovered, and told us her story. And, a chilling story it was, let me tell you. The army and police had pretty much ceased to exist by then, and they'd brought in a militia unit to restore order. Along with burning books and closing schools, they were herding people into confinement centers.

He paused and poured three glasses of

apple cider. After taking a sip, he continued his story.

"They weren't too organized at first, so we were able to rescue a few hundred, but that didn't last. Besides, we couldn't do much for people unless they were prepared to help themselves, and with the schools closed there wasn't much hope. But, Rebecca brought us hope. She told us about the efforts to save as much knowledge as possible by hiding books from the Library of Congress before the mobs burned them. Your grandfather was put in charge. She never knew the exact location he'd chosen – supposedly somewhere in one of the abandoned subway tunnels – but, he'd said he'd make sure the knowledge of that place was not only protected, but passed on. Apparently, he passed the information to his son, Ulysses, who passed it to you."

"Sure, I know where the books are," Hiroshi said. "But, I don't see how that helps you way out here."

Moses leaned forward, his voice lowered to just above a whisper.

"I'm going to share something with you, son," he said. "That not more than fifty people here in Freeland know. We have plans to invade New Liberty to get those books. With them we could start to restore the knowledge base that was lost when things fell apart. The only thing that's held us back is our not knowing just where in New Liberty the books are hidden."

"You would risk your lives just to find some books?" Clementine asked.

"You don't understand, young lady. Knowledge is power, real power. Oh, sure, you can control people with guns, but unless you possess more knowledge than the people you control, you risk them rising up against you. That's the main weakness of the city-states, because they don't allow education, you have the ignorant lording it over other ignorant people. It's a recipe for chaos and disaster eventually."

Hiroshi thought on what Moses was saying. He remembered how his knowledge of an ancient Chinese philosopher had allowed him to overcome the monitors despite their superior armament, and how knowing about bears had enabled him and Clementine to survive their encounter with the wild bear. Moses was right; the person with knowledge had the long-term advantage. Maybe it *was* worth the risk to gain access to the storehouse of knowledge hidden beneath New Liberty. But, he questioned whether or not he had it in him to take that risk.

"You said that most of the teachers escaped the cities and came here," Hiroshi said. "Don't they provide you with the knowledge you need?"

"They provide a lot, but most of them are very specialized. They can only tell us what they know. Besides, as they get older, their memory fades. No, we need a more general base of knowledge, and the hidden books have it."

It was becoming clear to Hiroshi where the conversation was going. He felt cold all over, and a bit lightheaded. His heart was pounding so hard he was sure the others could hear it, and he had a bit of difficulty breathing. Part of his mind said that this wasn't rational. He'd faced the monitors and the bear without hesitation, but now, just the thought of going back to New Liberty had him almost shaking. He forced himself to breathe deeply, sending his thoughts back to the times when he sat in a corner of the book cache, poring over the words that seemed to march across the page and into his mind. This calmed him a little, enough for him to begin to process what was happening. The monitors and the bear had been real dangers, things he could see and think of ways to deal with. Returning to New Liberty, though, was a completely different matter. He could only imagine what might happen, and it was the anticipation of the unknown that evoked his feelings of fear. The words of an American president, Franklin D. Roosevelt in his first address to a nation wracked by unemployment and economic collapse came to him, “The only thing we have to fear is fear itself.”

He knew that the only way he would be able to overcome this feeling was to face it head on.

“So,” he said. “I guess you’ll want me to lead you to the books?”

Before Moses could reply, his wife laid her hands on his shoulders.

“Before you answer that, Abraham,” she said. “You make sure this boy knows what you’re asking of him.”

Moses looked up at his wife, his eyes narrowed. Hiroshi saw a look pass between them that he could not interpret.

“All in good time, Sarah,” Moses said. “The first objective is to get as many of the books as we can.”

Clementine looked up at them. She placed her cup on the table and put her hands on her knees.

“You’re asking Hiroshi to go *back* to New Liberty? That’s awfully dangerous. The monitors would kill him on sight.” She shot a pleading glance at Hiroshi. “Tell me you’re not planning to go back there.”

"It is the best way," Hiroshi said. "I could try to tell them how to get to the books, but it's very complicated. It would be easier to *show* them, and I'd have to be there to do that."

Sarah Moses put her hands on her hips and glared down at her husband.

"You *have* to tell him, Abraham," she said. There was steel in her voice.

Abraham Moses sighed.

"I suppose you're right." He turned to Hiroshi. "Hiroshi, it *is* important to the continued survival of Freeland that we get those books, but as long as New Liberty remains as it is, even with the books we would be in danger."

"What are you suggesting, then?" Hiroshi asked.

"So far, the people of New Liberty haven't ventured far from their border fence," Moses said. "Human nature being what it is, however, we can't rely on that situation not changing. As their population grows, there will be pressure for more living space. If they should begin to expand, it's just a matter of time until they find us. We need to do something about them before that happens."

"But, what can you do?"

"Well, we know that the worker community, what you know as the proles, far outnumbers those in charge. While fear of the monitors' weapons is part of what keeps them in check, the real reason they submit to the tyranny is ignorance and lack of someone to rally them to resist. We've discussed this extensively, and the council believes that if we could show the proles an alternative way of life, they would rise up against those in charge."

Hiroshi's mind was racing. A small part resisted what he knew Moses was suggesting.

"You can't think that I would be able to get the prole community to resist the citizens and the monitors," he said.

"Son, revolutions have started with little more than an idea and someone with the ability to communicate it to others. You possess something that few others have – you have knowledge inside that head of yours, the knowledge of centuries. What's more, while you might not know it, the mere fact that you were able to escape from the monitors makes you a symbol of successful resistance. It's just a matter of getting that message to others."

The wheels in Hiroshi's head were spinning at full speed now. He was making the connections that he suspected Moses wanted him to make. It was true; he'd done what no prole before him had done; he'd gone up against the monitors and prevailed. He had escaped from New Liberty. If he stayed invisible, though, the impact of what he'd done would be lost, submerged in the incessant propaganda coming from the speakers all over the prole community. If, on the other hand, he returned, he would be a visible and potent symbol of possibilities, living proof that proles could in fact live free.

He looked around at the others. Abraham Moses eyed him with a hopeful expression, while his wife maintained a stoic look. Clementine's eyes were wide with fear, and her lips quivered. She laid a hand on his forearm. He could feel her shaking.

It was now left to him. *"Always remember."* His father's voice was clear in his mind. All those hours he'd spent among the stacks of books, the time of poring over words to puzzle out their meanings, staring at pictures of scenes that represented a world that he thought he would never know except in him mind, had been, at the time, just an interesting way for a precocious child to pass the time. He now knew differently. His father had been preparing him, and even though he didn't live to see it, Hiroshi was determined that his effort would not be in vain.

The queasiness of fear had drifted away,

to be replaced with a feeling of steely resolve. It was a strange sensation, like nothing he'd ever felt before.

"Okay," he said. "I'll do it."

# 19.

## *New Liberty*

The Committee was gathered. All were in their customary places, and all eyes were focused on the Chairman.

Gravius-One, his ebony face impassive, sat facing Hector Cruz. Unlike everyone else present, he knew the reason for the Chairman's scowl. Inwardly, he was amused at the thought of the others worrying that Cruz's wrath might fall on them for some infraction, real or imagined. Drake Edison looked particularly concerned, no doubt because the escape of a prole, while it was directly linked to poor performance on the part of Gravius's monitors, nonetheless impacted on poor Edison's population control ministry, and the poor man knew how Cruz dealt with failure.

Cruz looked at the faces around the table. Inwardly, he was fuming, but he'd finally managed to get his anger under control. Control - that was the key. He must never, ever lose control. His father had let control slip from his fingers, allowing the other Committee members too much say in events, and that had been his undoing. Cruz was determined not to suffer the same fate. Of course, he often thought, he didn't have a son waiting in the wings for him to make a mistake, only these vultures sitting around the table, not one of whom, with the possible exception of Gravius, with the balls or guts to do anything but wait, unlike him. He'd acted when action was necessary – but, that was another issue, now, he had to deal with a more immediate issue.

His gaze came to rest on the monitor commander. *This one,* he thought, *I will have to watch closely. Right now he's essential to my plans, but there will come a day when he will be too great a liability, and I'll have to think of a way to eliminate him.*

"Citizens," he said. "We're faced with a crisis." He chose each word carefully. He wanted them worried, but unsure at the same time. "A prole not only killed two of our monitors, but escaped from New Liberty. We've clamped down on the information, but you know as well as I that such things can't be kept hidden forever."

Jebediah Robertson smiled wolfishly at the dismayed looking Edison. The elder, though a man of the cloth, wasn't immune from the effects of sitting so close to the center of power. He didn't think much of Edison, thought Cruz was a spoiled brat, and Wainwright a pompous jackass. The dark-skinned monitor commander, Gravius, was the only one he came close to respecting, but it was a respect born out of fear. For now, he satisfied himself with enjoying Edison's discomfort.

"If word gets out that a prole did such a thing and went unpunished, you could have problems, Citizen Edison," he said.

Edison's cheeks flamed crimson.

"There have been no problems among the workers," he said. "Besides, it was poor performance of the monitors that caused this, not anything my ministry did." He glared at Gravius-One who studiously ignored him.

Cruz noticed this byplay, and what he saw worried him. Gravius was like a large statue carved from some obsidian rock. He never seemed bothered as the others did, nor did he engage in the back and forth sniping as they did in their pathetic attempts to either impress him or to cut each other down. As the alpha male of the pack, Cruz knew that the only threat to his dominance would come from the monitor commander – the true alpha male. He needed to begin the process of taking Gravius down a peg or two, but it had to be done skillfully. He wasn't quite ready to alienate him entirely.

"He has a point, Citizen Gravius," Cruz said. "A single prole, and a mere child at that, overcame two of your armed men. How do you expect to maintain control over the population with such shoddy performance?"

He flavored his words with a smile that to Gravius looked like a cat about to pounce upon an unsuspecting bird.

"You make an excellent point, Citizen Cruz," Gravius responded levelly. "Rest assured that the officer that sent the monitors out who botched this job has been dealt with." The officer in charge of the station had been demoted and assigned duty as guard at the manure processing facility near the power plant, and had been lucky that Gravius hadn't executed him on the spot. "The two monitors, of course, paid for their stupidity and incompetence. The situation has been contained."

"That, at least, is gratifying to hear, citizen, but what have you done to prepare for the possibility of prole unrest when, and I believe it just a matter of time, the word gets out that your much-vaunted monitors are not so powerful after all?"

"I wouldn't worry over much about that, citizen," Gravius said in his gravelly voice. "The death of two monitors at the hands of a prole, and the punishment visited upon the officer in charge of that debacle has focused every monitor's attention on the need for vigilance. A prole even looking cross-eyed at a monitor at the moment is likely to be shredded on the spot. Don't worry, we have things under control."

Cruz's smile broadened. As much as he feared Gravius, he also admired the man's iron self-control.

"That is good to hear, my friend, good indeed. Now, on to other business." He turned to Edison. "Are plans for the culling still on track?"

"Y-yes, citizen, everything is in order. Those who were not already in custody were picked up and transported without incident – except for the one prole from Columbus Heights."

"Was there indication that anyone knew of the situation with the prole Hiroshi Jackson?"

"No --," Edison started to say, but was cut off by a preemptory wave of Gravius-One's hand.

"When the monitors arrived at the Columbus Heights Crèche, there was some concern about Jackson having been picked up the night before off schedule," Gravius said. "And, the director reported that another prole, Clementine Adams, was also missing, but when the monitor officer in charge of the detail told her that both had been taken into custody, she seemed mollified. I'm sure no one knows except us." *"Us, and every monitor on the force by now."*

"What about the presence of two dead monitors on the premises?" Cruz asked.

"Fortunately, we were able to get into the facility and remove the bodies before any of the residents became aware of their presence. No one seemed to be aware that anything other than the unscheduled pickup had occurred."

*"You have an answer for everything,"* Cruz thought. *"Or, so you think. But, you don't know what's on my mind, and that will be your undoing."* "Very good, citizen," he said. "I am concerned, however, that your monitors terminated the search for these two proles so early." Gravius opened his mouth to speak, but Cruz held up a hand. "I know - the assumption is that they perished in the wilds, or were eaten by animals. A dangerous

assumption, I assure you, especially where this prole Jackson is concerned. I want the search resumed, and I don't want to hear that it has been terminated until you can bring Jackson for me to see. If he has been killed by animals, I want to see the corpse."

# 20.

The others had long since filed from the room, confused looks on their faces. None of them more so than the monitor commander, who he had ordered to resume the search for the two missing proles. That had given him a certain amount of pleasure, knowing that Gravius had wanted to refuse, but dared not.

Cruz sat staring at the empty chairs, his mind in turmoil. The others might not understand why a single prole boy could be so important, but he did. He should have had the child killed with his parents. But, he had allowed his spiritual advisor, Elder Robertson, to talk him into putting the boy in a crèche. Robertson and his damned book, and his rules and restrictions. He would be among the first to go, right after the monitor commander, as soon as Cruz had his hands on those missing books.

His last encounter with Ulysses Jackson still rankled. He'd handled it badly by allowing his emotions to rule.

It had been eleven years earlier, and in this very room.

When the monitors brought Ulysses and Junko to him, it was clear that they'd been beaten, and beaten badly. Junko Jackson's left eye was swollen shut, and Ulysses' right ear was hanging from his skull by a thread of tissue. Despite their injuries, both looked at Cruz with derision as they were shoved toward him.

"You're probably wondering why I had you brought here," Cruz said.

Ulysses' lips were swollen, making it difficult for him to speak, but he was able to spit a glob of bloody sputum in Cruz's direction.

"Iss proly 'cause you want to wash us die, you bastard," he muttered through his misshapened lips.

Cruz laughed; a sound completely without mirth.

"Hardly, Ulysses," he said. "After all, we grew up together. You were like a brother to me." He looked at Junko. "And, you know how I felt about you."

She turned her head away, refusing to meet his gaze.

"If he's like a brother, and you care so much about me," she said with venom in her voice. "Why did you have us beaten like this?"

"I'm afraid the monitors were perhaps a bit over zealous. But, you were in violation of the law. You know that all births are supposed to be registered and the children delivered to a crèche for orientation. You kept that brat of yours hidden for seven years."

Junko stood erect with her shoulders back, and turned to face Cruz directly. The look of hatred that clouded her beautiful features gave him a hollow feeling in his chest. His cheeks felt hot.

"Hector Cruz," she said coldly. "I was not about to turn my child over to the *state* to be raised as a mindless, docile worker in the factory. What The Committee is doing to the prole community is nothing less than slavery to allow a few citizens to live in idle comfort."

"Ah, my beautiful Junko. You always were the fiery one. But, you can't put yourself above the community. The will of the individual must always be subordinate to that of the collective."

She made a snorting sound, and then

winced in pain.

"Except the will of the collective is really the will of the Cruz family," she said. "You rule the citizens through coercion and who knows what, and you rule the prole community by keeping the ignorant and backing it up with the weapons of the monitors. In the meantime, none of the rules seem to apply to you, or the select few close to you."

*"At one time, you and this fool, Ulysses, were among the select few,"* Cruz thought. "You could have enjoyed that privilege as well, my dear," he said. "Instead, you chose to follow Ulysses here on his foolish mission to bring enlightenment to the proles."

Ulysses Jackson moved to place himself between Cruz and Junko. He stared down at the man he had once called friend.

"Stop playing with us, Hector," he said slowly and painfully through his swollen lips. "Tell us why you had us brought here instead of executed."

"Good old Ulysses," Cruz said. "I could never hide anything from you, could I? Very well, I'll tell you. I could have you executed – after all it is the law – but I'm willing to offer you clemency."

"At what price?"

"Your father was involved in removing forbidden texts from the Library of Congress during the purges and hiding them somewhere. Unfortunately, he was killed during the final assault and The Committee was never able to interrogate him to locate that hiding place." Cruz looked up at Ulysses with eyes that were cold and lifeless. "At the time, it was assumed that the location died with him, and, while my father believed it, I never did. I was . . . am convinced that Benjamin Jackson shared the hiding place with someone – and, that someone, Ulysses, is you. I'd hoped you might lead me to it someday, but you turned out to be like your father. I've had you watched since you went back over the river, but I must say, you're quite skillful. My spies have never been able to track you to the books."

"Maybe, that's because they don't exist," Ulysses said.

"Oh, but we both know that they do. And, I mean to have them, so here's my deal – tell me where they are and I'll spare the two of you. I might even allow you access to that whelp of yours – provided you agree not to make a fuss about him being in the crèche."

"If I did know where such books were hidden – and, I'm not saying that I do - why would I tell you so that could be destroyed?" Ulysses' eyes widened. "Because, you have no intention of destroying them, do you? You want them and the knowledge they contain for yourself."

"What's wrong with that? Besides, if you tell me, you and your beautiful Junko here get to live."

Ulysses was torn. Like anyone, he wanted to live, and he certainly didn't want Junko to die. But, the thought of living in a world where monsters like Hector Cruz had all the power was repellent. His father had entrusted him with the secret of knowledge. He could not betray that trust.

"Sorry, Hector," he said. "I can't help you."

"You mean you won't help me."

Ulysses stared back, his expression wooden.

*"All right, then,"* Cruz thought. *"You want to die, so be it."*

He looked over at the two monitors who'd been standing motionless just inside the door. He nodded and waved his hand negligently.

The monitors marched over.

"Take them out and execute them," he said without emotion.

The monitors took the prisoners by the

arms and pulled them from the room. Cruz sat alone, brooding, for hours after they'd gone.

Just as he brooded now, thinking back to that evening. At the time, he'd not considered the possibility that Ulysses might have shared the secret with his seven-year-old son. That had been his mistake. He'd allowed his anger and jealousy to override his common sense. He could at least have used the boy as leverage against him if Robertson hadn't forbidden it, insisting that the child must be taken immediately to a crèche.

Now, he had to find Hiroshi Jackson if he was to achieve his aims.

# 21.

As they came down the mountain in their approach to the river crossing, Hiroshi was beginning to have second thoughts.

After agreeing to help Abraham Moses and the Freelanders in their campaign against New Liberty, he'd spent time with Rebecca Stennis learning more about his family history. He'd been impressed at the bravery shown by his grandparents, and their heroic efforts to preserve knowledge in the face of the ignorance that was running rampant as the economy and ecology of the world began falling apart and people reverted to barbarism. He knew that his father had inherited that bravery and dedication. As he and the small group of Freelanders hiked through the forests and mountains north and west of New Liberty, he began to wonder if he'd inherited it as well.

Hiroshi, Abraham, and ten men had left the settlement before sunrise, and had reached the river crossing by dark. They camped on the west side and crossed at sunrise the next morning. Across the river, they began moving south and southeast, planning to approach New Liberty from the north, parallel the fence to the river, and then infiltrate under the fence near where Hiroshi and Clementine had made their escape.

Away from the mountains the temperatures were higher, and they were very quickly covered in sweat. Even though the terrain was relatively level, because of the heat and humidity, walking required some effort, so they stopped frequently. Near mid-day, as they were an estimated three hours from the river, they stopped in a clearing on a slight rise.

Most of the men found shaded spots under large bushes or against the trunks of trees, while Abraham Moses assigned five to sentry duty in a circle around the clearing.

"Is that really necessary?" Hiroshi asked.

"We're not too far from New Liberty," Moses said. "While they don't normally patrol out this far, with you and Clementine escaping, we have to assume they'll be on extra alert, and they might still be looking for you."

Hiroshi hadn't thought of that.

"That could make it difficult to get to the place where the books are hidden," he said.

"Well, you two managed to get out. It's doubtful they'll be looking for you inside the fence. Once we get through, we only have to find a place to hide until dark."

Hiroshi had to admit that made sense. Of course, getting to the fence wouldn't be a cake walk.

As if he'd mentally summoned them, they saw four black-suited monitors thrashing noisily through the brush about a half mile away and downhill from them.

"Shouldn't be too hard to avoid them out here," Hiroshi said. "You can hear them from a mile away. They make more noise than an angry bear."

This brought a laugh from everyone in the clearing.

"You have a point, but it's not good to under estimate your opponent, as you well know."

They waited until the monitors were well away and heading west before continuing their journey toward the river. On the way they spotted two more groups of monitors. Moving cautiously, it was nearing sundown by the time they reached the river, and almost dark before they made their way to where the fence went into the river.

Moses had them wait in the bushes for several hours just to make sure the area wasn't being patrolled. When he decided it was safe to move, he and Hiroshi moved down the muddy river bank along the fence. Hiroshi found the rusted wires he'd broken in his own escape, and bent them back. He bent back two more to make more space, as Moses and some of the men were much bulkier than either him or Clementine.

After everyone had made it through the wire, Hiroshi led them up the bank and eastward toward the edge of the prole community. The smell of burning methane and animal manure used as fertilizer was strong in the air, making his eyes sting and tear up. He'd gotten used to the clean air of Freeland, and forgotten just how noxious New Liberty's atmosphere was. The others suffered even more, having never been subjected to this level of pollution.

"How the hell does anyone live in this muck," one of the men, a light browned skinned man with slick black hair, said. "It smells worse than a privy before you put lime in it."

"Quiet," Moses said in a harsh whisper.

"Just because you don't see anyone about, doesn't mean there's no one about."

"The monitors don't often patrol the streets at night," Hiroshi said. "They guard the entrances to the factories and other buildings. Few people go outside at night."

"Can't blame them for that," the dark-haired man said in a tone just above a whisper. "At least inside the smell might not be as bad."

When they came to the first buildings, Hiroshi led them through the alleyways, avoiding the main streets. It took the better part of an hour for him to find the iron grating in the park half a mile the vine-covered building that had once housed most of the world's knowledge. The grating was near the center of the park and under a tangle of thorns and English ivy. He hadn't been to this place since he was seven, but it didn't seem changed from his last visit.

With Moses' help, Hiroshi hefted the grate out of place and, stepping onto the rusty metal ladder, slipped down into the tunnel it covered. The others followed. At the bottom of the ladder, he felt his way along the wall until he came to a T-intersection, where he turned left. He led the others about twenty feet and stopped, feeling around the wall until he found the recess about three feet up from the floor in which his father stashed the torches he'd so laboriously fashioned from certain twigs and branches found in the park above. Hiroshi took out two torches, handing one to Moses. The Freelander lit them.

With the flickering torches leading the way, Hiroshi and Moses led the ten men along the underground tunnel which twisted and turned several times before terminating at a large, rectangular metal door that looked rusted into its frame.

"How do we get through that?" Moses asked.

Hiroshi studied the door, trying to recall how his father had opened it. He felt along the seam between door and frame. About midway down, he felt a slight bump in the metal. He remembered his father holding his hand in about this same position and the door swinging inward. He pressed the bump, and was rewarded with a grinding sound as the metal door swung open.

Hiroshi walked through, followed by the others. As the light of the two torches illuminated the space, there were gasps of astonishment. Before them was row upon row of books, stacked neatly.

"My God," Moses said. "I've heard of it for years, and I never really doubted, but to stand here and look at it . . . it's . . . amazing.

And, to think, Hiroshi, you grew up surrounded by all this knowledge."

Hiroshi looked around. He felt the hot sting of tears as he recalled the times he'd spent here with his father, at first learning to read, and later reading on his own.

"Yeah," he said. "It's been a long time, but everything is exactly like I remembered it."

"Okay," Moses said. "We don't have much time." He turned to the others, each of whom had an empty pack. "You each have your instructions on what kind of book to get. Fill the packs as quickly as you can."

"What do you want me to do?" Hiroshi asked.

Moses put a hand on Hiroshi's shoulder.

"Well, I was thinking we might start our campaign against The Committee. It'd be nice if we could have you talk to someone in the community, you know, let them know you're still alive. That might start word spreading that the monitors aren't all that powerful."

"I suppose I could go to the crèche and talk to my friend Washington. He could spread the word, both at the crèche and during work detail."

"Good, we'll go and do that." He turned to the others. "When you're finished, make your way back to the other side of the fence. Hiroshi and I will catch up to you as soon as we can."

The two of them then made their way in the dark back to the grate. Moses made sure to put it back in place and cover it with foliage. He then followed Hiroshi to the west and south to the vicinity of the Columbus Heights Crèche. Hiroshi signaled a halt in a narrow alley about two blocks west of the facility.

"Wait here," he whispered. "I know a way in without being seen. I'll go in and talk to Washington."

"I should go with you," Moses said. "We don't want anything happening to you now."

"No, it would be better if I went alone. Don't worry; I know every nook and cranny of that place. I can get in and out without being seen."

Moses relented. He found a hiding place in a recess where a small hip wall had been built out from the building's main wall.

"Okay," he said to Hiroshi as he prepared to leave. "You need to get in and out in an hour. We want to be over the fence and far away from here before sunrise."

Hiroshi nodded and, edging along the walls and keeping in the shadows, he walked to his old home.

He made his way around to the rear of the building where the trash bins were kept. A dark, seldom visited area, it had, along with the roof, been a place where Hiroshi, Washington, and Clementine had often met. The door had a lock, but he had long ago learned how to jiggle it to release the bolt. He did it as quietly and quickly as ever, and slipped into the dim hallway. It was nearing midnight, and the facility was quiet as he made his way through the building to the sleeping area. He eased through the door, passed a few sleep cubicles from which he could hear the sound of snoring or deep breathing, and came to the area near the back where he and Washington Benedict had slept for many years. In the dim light from a window set high up on the wall, he saw his friend huddled under the thin blanket. The adjacent cot, where he once slept, was empty.

Hiroshi knelt near the head of the cot and laid a hand softly on his sleeping friend's shoulder.

"Wash, wake up," he whispered.

The boy turned over, making a low moaning sound. His eyes opened. He stared up into Hiroshi's face, blinking rapidly and shaking his head. Then, as his vision cleared, his eyes opened wide and he started to open his mouth. Hiroshi quickly clamped a hand over his mouth.

"No, don't say anything," he whispered urgently.

Washington nodded. Hiroshi slowly withdrew his hand.

"They told us you were dead," he whispered hoarsely.

"Well," Hiroshi said. "That's obviously not true. Get up and come with me, and I'll explain everything."

Washington pulled the blanket back and got out of bed. He was wearing shorts and a T-shirt. Barefoot, he followed Hiroshi back through the building. In the back room, Hiroshi placed a hand on his chest, stopping him near the door.

"Okay, Hirosh," Washington said. "What the hell's going on, and where's Clementine?"

Huddling close, Hiroshi told his friend what had happened from the time Octavia Olympus had summoned him to her office. He ended his tale with his and Clementine's escape from New Liberty.

"But, she's okay," he said. "She's being taken good care of."

"By who?" Washington demanded.

"Hirosh, how could you put her in a situation like that? You could have gotten her killed."

"Hey, it wasn't like I planned it. How was I to know they'd come for me early? It just happened, you know, and we had no choice but to run. I couldn't leave her here after we killed those two monitors."

Washington Benedict was angry with Hiroshi for endangering Clementine, which was clear from his expression. But, he was also impressed that his friends had beaten not one but two armed monitors.

"You two got away from the monitors," he said. There was awe, mixed with anger in his voice. "Why did you come back? You know they'll be looking for you."

"I came back because people have to know they're lying. They also have to know that the monitors aren't as powerful as they try to make us believe. You've got to let people know, Wash. We don't have to live like slaves anymore if we don't want to."

"But, if they catch you, they'll kill you and make it look like they just found the body. We can't beat the monitors, Hirosh, you know that."

"I don't know any such thing." Now, there was anger in Hiroshi's voice. "I only know that they've been lying to us for all these years, and using us like animals or machines. They didn't kill me the first time, and they won't this time. You just let people know I'm still alive. I have to go now, but I'll be back."

With that, Hiroshi slipped through the door and started along the wall toward the place he'd left Moses. He didn't see his friend frown and then turn and head toward the front of the building. He didn't see him talking to the monitor who stood guard at the front door. Had it not been that his senses were on high alert after his visit to the cache of books, he wouldn't have heard the footfalls of the monitor who came around the side of the building, heading in his direction.

The scraping sound was just on the edge of his consciousness at first. Just a slight noise that seemed out of place. He quickly recognized the noise as footsteps, and that they were getting closer. He hugged the wall and slowly turned to look back the way he'd come. The monitor, in his black suit, was almost invisible at first, but he wasn't being as careful as Hiroshi, so he didn't walk close to the wall. Hiroshi saw the shadow as the monitor moved through pools of dim light where the full moon peeked through gaps in the clouds and smog.

*"Damn,"* he thought. *"He must be the guard from the front. He might have heard me*

*coming out. I hope Wash doesn't get into any trouble."*

He couldn't help his friend, especially if the monitor captured him. He also didn't want to endanger Moses and the others. That left him with only one option. He darted from the wall, and ran across the street, away from where Moses was hiding.

"Halt, prole," the monitor shouted.

Before the man could draw and fire his flechette pistol, Hiroshi had plunged into the darkness of the alley across the street, and was running full speed. He only hoped that Moses had seen what was happening and would make his way to the fence and freedom. He prayed that *he* would be able to elude the pursuing monitor and get there himself.

# 22.

Octavia Olympus arrived at the crèche early, only to find the place in chaos.

Black-uniformed monitors were all over the entry area, with children of all ages lined up along the walls being interrogated. Some of the younger children were crying, while the older ones looked sullen and angry at the treatment they were receiving. Her attendants stood by with helpless expressions.

She walked up to the monitor who seemed to be in charge.

"Excuse me, citizen," she said coldly. "Do you mind telling me why you and your men are inside this facility without my permission?"

The man, fully a foot taller than Olympus, turned to face her. As was the custom when addressing citizens, he lifted his visor, revealing a broad-cheeked, ruddy face and dark blue eyes.

"Are you Citizen Olympus, the head of this facility?" he asked in a deep voice.

"Yes, I am. Now, will you tell me why you're here? I gave no permission for monitors to enter this crèche."

"Citizen, under Article 17 of New Liberty law, I don't need permission to enter a structure when a crime is being committed, or when a criminal is present or has been present in that structure. A wanted felon was reported in this facility last night. My men and I have entered to question the residents to see if anyone saw this felon, or perhaps helped him."

"A f-felon – were any of the chil-, er, residents, hurt?"

The monitor turned away, watching one of his men nearby as he ushered the children he'd been talking to away.

"That's not my problem, citizen," he said. "I'm here to track the felon down, who, by the way, was a former resident."

Olympus' eyes widened and she frowned.

"That's impossible. I would know if any of my, the residents, were wanted by the authorities, and there is no one in that category since I became director of this facility."

"There are *two* wanted felons who are recent residents," he said. "Hiroshi Jackson and Clementine Adams; do you remember them?"

She took a step backwards, her hands going to her throat. Her already pallid complexioned became even more waxen.

"B-but, that's impossible. Hi . . . the two of them were taken from here by your own people just a few days ago."

The monitor remained impassive. He had a job to do, and wasn't interested in the pallid woman's views.

"That is incorrect, citizen," he said. "They killed the two monitors who came for them, and escaped. One of your residents reported to the monitor on sentry duty that the felon Hiroshi Jackson came back last night. The monitor gave chase, but he escaped again. Oh, and should you repeat any of this, you will be in violation of security regulations, and subject to arrest – am I clear on that?"

Olympus stood there, her arms limply at her sides, staring at a point beyond the man's head. She nodded dumbly. What he'd just said hit her like a blow to the stomach. On the one hand, she was happy to hear that

Hiroshi and Clementine had escaped – the two of them had always been her favorites. On the other, she was shocked to learn that they'd killed, and monitors at that. She had never thought either of them capable of violence.

There was, of course, nothing she could do. The monitors had the law and The Committee on their side, and not even a citizen was above the law. She had done what would be expected of someone in her position, but to continue to challenge the monitor in the performance of his duties would look suspicious. She was curious, though, to know the identity of the resident who had reported Hiroshi's presence. She couldn't ask the monitor. That would be information she wasn't entitled to have. Then, she thought of Washington Benedict. He was friends with both Hiroshi and Clementine. He might perhaps know.

She inclined her head slightly, acknowledging the monitor's presence and demonstrating her obedience to the protocols. Then, she turned and walked slowly away, heading toward the sleeping area. She hadn't seen Washington among those being questioned by the monitors, and assumed he would still be in the sleeping area.

She walked slowly past the monitors and the children. The former ignored her. As far as they were concerned, she was no more than part of the furnishings. That was the essence of the monitors, young men recruited from the citizen crèches when they turned sixteen, and taken to the monitor training school where they were stripped of their surnames and given numbers, and then turned into emotionless automatons. The children - and she found herself more and more thinking of them not as proles but just children - avoided her eyes as she passed. This too she understood. She was part of the system that treated them as economic production units instead of human beings. Even though, with each passing day, her own conditioning was weakening, she had tried to keep her emotional distance when interacting with them. It was the only way she could maintain her sanity. Now, though, it all seemed to be slipping away.

The hum of conversations, as the monitors asked their questions and the children answered in monosyllables, along with the drone of trite phrases about the 'primacy of the community' from the loudspeakers that were affixed at regular intervals along the top of the walls throughout most of the facility, followed her as she made her way from the entrance foyer, past the dining facility, to the sleeping area.

As she'd expected, she found Washington Benedict in the sleeping area. He sat on his cot, his back against the wall, and his head propped on his knees. As she approached, she could see that his body was shaking.

"Mr. Benedict," she said. "Is something wrong?"

He looked up, a startled expression on his brown face. His cheeks were streaked with tears.

"Uh . . . no . . . headmaster. I . . . I . . . just wasn't feeling well." He stared at his knees.

She sat on the foot of the cot, facing him.

"Are you sure?" She reached over and placed a hand on his. "There are monitors outside. Did they talk to you?"

"No, they haven't talked to me," he said. He continued to look down at his knees.

"Washington, you know you should never try to lie to me. I always know when someone is lying. You, for instance, you can't look me in the eye right now. That's a sure sign you're lying. Now, what did the monitors ask you? Did they ask about Hiroshi and Clementine?"

"Hiroshi and Clementine? I . . . uh . . . why would they be asking about them?"

"Because they're still alive, and they escaped from the monitors," she said. "And,

Hiroshi was here last night."

His mouth dropped open.

"Uh, how did you know that?" he asked.

"The question is, how did *you* know?" Then, it hit her, and she found it hard to believe. "Are you the one who told them?" she asked, hoping he'd say no, but somehow knowing he wouldn't.

His face fell, and he started shaking and crying harder.

She moved up on the bed and put her arms around his shoulder, gently massaging his back. His body shook in her arms, and she could feel the wetness of his tears on her shoulder.

"I d-didn't mean to," he said between sobs. "I d-don't know why I d-did it. I just did."

"There, there," she said. "It's all right."

He pulled back from her, his face contorted.

"No, it's not all right," he almost shouted. "I told on him. It was me that told the monitors that Hiroshi was here. They'll kill him because of me."

"Don't worry, he's not dead yet."

"How do you know that?"

"I just know," she said. "I just know."

# 23.

Hiroshi ran all night. He ran to the river. Getting under the fence, he tore the shirt Rebecca Stennis had given him back in Freeland, and dug a furrow in his shoulder, which stung like hell for hours afterwards. Once under the fence and back up the river bank, he ran on. He ran until his lungs burned and he felt like he would drop from exhaustion. First he ran west, following along the river, and then he turned north, generally following the same route he and Clementine had used during his first escape from New Liberty.

His body finally began to flag just as the sky was beginning to lighten in the east. He had no idea how far he'd run, but he kept putting one foot in front of another, weaving from side to side, and occasionally bumping into trees. His vision was blurring and he felt a throbbing just above his temples.

In a bend in the trail, just as he began swinging around a large tree, his forward foot caught in a root that protruded a half inch above the surface of the earth. He pitched forward, landing face first, his mouth filling with dirt and leaves.

He sputtered and spit to clear his mouth, and then lay there, his chin on the ground, breathing noisily. His chest felt as if it was on fire. For a moment, all he wanted to do was close his eyes and sleep. But, he knew he had to get up, had to keep moving. He couldn't stop now. Slowly, painfully, he began to lever himself up.

As his head came up, a strange looking apparition appeared before his eyes. His vision was blurred, causing the figure to waver and shimmer. It looked like a small bear at first, but then slowly his vision cleared, and he saw that it was even worse than a bear. A monitor, dressed in black from head to foot, a visor covering his face, stood athwart the trail, his flechette pistol aimed at Hiroshi's head.

Hiroshi felt like a slowly deflating balloon. The air leaked from his lungs in a slow hiss. He'd pushed his body to the limits, survived two brushes with the monitors, found a new life, only to die because he'd fallen on his face in the forest right at the foot of a monitor who probably couldn't find his way back to New

Liberty on his own. Rather than fear, though, he only felt disgust and disappointment.

He had, at least, led the Freelanders to the books. Moses would remember the directions, and Hiroshi had no doubt that there would be more late night visits by the Freelanders, retrieving the precious texts. Moreover, Washington would spread the word that he'd been back in New Liberty, so, even in death he might serve as a rallying point for resistance to those across the river.

He'd made it onto his knees, but fatigue won out. He could rise no further. He hated the thought that he would die on his knees, but was determined not to beg for his life. He didn't, however, want his last sight to be that of the faceless symbol of his oppression, so he closed his eyes and summoned up an image of Clementine, his lovely Clementine.

Hiroshi waited for the ripping sound of the flechette gun, to be followed by a moment of intense pain as dozens of the steel darts tore into and through his flesh, and then oblivion. He found that rather than dreading it, he faced it calmly. But, all he heard was the tweeting and cawing of early morning birds seeking food and the sigh of a soft wind blowing through the leaves, a wind that warmly caressed his cheeks.

Then, he heard the sound of boots

scuffing the hard packed earth upon which he knelt, and the thump of something hard impacting the ground a few feet to his front. Slowly, he opened his eyes.

The monitor, now with his jacket and helmet removed, stood there looking at Hiroshi, an expression of bewilderment on his youthful face. The flechette pistol was pointed at the ground.

"Who are you?" the monitor asked. "Are you one of the Wild Ones?"

## 24.

Hiroshi stared in amazement at the man in front of him – actually, he thought; boy might be more accurate, as the monitor didn't look that much older than he was.

*"He looks like I must have looked when I first met Abraham and the others,"* he thought. *"He's probably never been this far away from New Liberty before, and he's lost – lost and scared."*

The monitor was not only looking lost, but the way his eyes kept darting around, as if he was expecting company, Hiroshi saw that he *was* afraid.

*"He thinks I'm part of a larger group, I'll bet, and is worried that they're close by. That's probably the only reason he hasn't shot*

*me.”*

Hiroshi realized that the man didn’t recognize him. But, then, he wouldn’t, because proles of New Liberty wore only the drab singlesuits, and he was dressed in a blue and green shirt that had been made by one of Freeland’s tailors, and a pair of pants that Abraham had given him. The monitors out here on the frontier probably wouldn’t have a description beyond ‘missing prole.’ Had he been wearing a singlesuit, no more description would be needed.

“Are you one of the Wild Ones?” the monitor asked again.

“We call ourselves Freelanders, and we’re not wild,” Hiroshi said, making an effort to sound tough and authoritative. “You’re from New Liberty. What’s your name, and what are *you* doing this far away from *your* home?”

The boy’s Adam’s apple bobbled as he looked nervously from Hiroshi to the surrounding forest.

“I’m Leland-27,” he said. “I was part of a team looking for a fugitive from New Liberty. Last night, some big animal, attacked us as we passed through the trees. It killed Godfrey-12 with one swipe of its arm, or leg, or whatever.” Hiroshi realized that he was describing an encounter with a bear. “The rest of us ran for our lives, and I got separated from the group, and now I'm lost. Can you tell me the way to New Liberty?"

*"I was right,"* Hiroshi thought. *"He is lost."* "I'm sorry, Leland," he said. "I don't know the way to New Liberty. But, I can take you with me to Freeland."

Leland-27's eyes widened and his face drained of color.

"Uh, I don't know . . . I've . . . heard . . . that --"

Hiroshi held up a hand. "I know. You've heard that the people of Freeland, those you call the Wild Ones, will kill anyone from New Liberty, especially if they happen to be a monitor."

The monitor's eyes went from wide in fear to narrow in suspicion.

"How do you know what I am?"

"We see those of your kind here in the forest from time to time," Hiroshi said. "Though, not usually this far out." He realized that it was dangerous to betray too much knowledge of New Liberty, at least until he was back with the others. "We've heard them talking. You are part of the organization that provides security for your community, are you not?"

"Uh, yes, I am," Leland-27 said, somewhat

mollified. "If I went with you, do you think someone could help me get back home?"

"I believe that would be possible," Hiroshi said. *"But, I seriously doubt anyone will volunteer, or that when you experience Freeland you'll want to go back."*

Slowly so as to avoid more pain, Hiroshi levered himself upright. "Okay, Leland," he said, brushing dirt and debris from his clothing. "It is okay if I call you Leland, isn't it?" Leland nodded. "I'll guide you to Freeland, and we'll see if someone can help you. You were wise to remove your jacket and headgear. Some in Freeland have had bad encounters with your kind."

Leland nodded.

"I figured as much. I haven't been on duty outside the fence for long, but I've heard stories about what you wild, er, Freelanders, do to monitors."

He stepped aside as Hiroshi advanced and pointed to the west. "We go this way," Hiroshi said. "I think we have about half a day's walking. By the way, I'm curious about something. Why didn't you shoot me when I was helpless on the ground?"

Leland shook his head.

"I don't know," he said. "I wasn't sure you were alone. I'm lost and thought you might be able to help me find my way. And, oh, it just didn't seem right to shoot a person who was helpless like that."

"I thought you monitors were trained to be without feeling."

"I, uh, well, yes, that is part of our training. But, I was assigned to the Chairman's security detail immediately after training. That was good duty, but I saw how the citizens lived. It didn't make much impact until the accident that got me posted out here. I guess I started to question a lot of what I've been taught."

Hiroshi didn't say anything, but his mind was racing. If a monitor could come to doubt the system of New Liberty, maybe there was hope that the proles could be convinced to rise up against it. He hoped that Washington was already spreading the word that he was alive and had successfully faced down the monitors.

"Well, Leland, I think you will find Freeland an interesting place to be."

# 25.

Hiroshi and Leland-27 crossed the river just after midday. They were no more than an hour's walk from the crossing when they caught up with Abraham Moses and the others.

Hiroshi's reunion with his friends was joyous.

Moses rushed up and pulled Hiroshi into a bear hug as the others crowded around, patting him on the back.

"Hiroshi," Moses said. "I was beginning to worry about you, but I guess I should know better, eh. If there's anyone who can survive out here, it'd have to be you, having already escaped New Liberty once."

Everyone had ignored Leland-27 until he pushed forward to confront Hiroshi.

"He called you Hiroshi," he said. "Are you -"

"Yes, I am Hiroshi Jackson."

Moses stepped back, eying Leland.

"And, who might this be, Hiroshi?" he asked with a wary, but menacing tone.

Hiroshi looked at the young monitor. The man's face was pale again, and his eyes darted from one to another of the eleven men who now surrounded him.

"This is Leland-27," Hiroshi said. "He found me in the forest after I fell down and stayed with me to keep me safe."

Moses still looked warily at the newcomer. "Is that so, now? Well, Leland-27, that's a strange name you have, and I notice that you're wearing one of those pistols that the monitors of New Liberty wear. Would you by any chance be a monitor?"

The others moved in closer, murmuring. Leland-27 paled even more.

"He was running away from the monitors when he found me," Hiroshi said, moving to stand next to him. "I think he was trying to escape form New Liberty, too. If he wasn't, why do you think he didn't just kill me where he found me?"

Moses rubbed his hand through his beard. He cocked his head and looked down at Hiroshi.

"Now, you do have a point there, Hiroshi," he said. "Okay, young fellow, is what Hiroshi says true? Are you running away from the monitors?"

Leland-27 looked from Hiroshi to the giant bearded man, and then at the others who still regarded him with naked hostility. Even with his flechette pistol, he was no match for so many. The man's question intrigued him, too. *Was* he running away from the monitors? Did he really want to go back to New Liberty, where he would still be assigned to external patrol for fear that the Chairman might, if he should catch sight of him, still want him executed, and where he would now be the butt of even more jokes and hazing? Or, even worse, would he return to an atmosphere of suspicion because of his exposure to the world outside the sterile, controlled environment of New Liberty? These people regarded him with suspicion and hostility, but he was after all a stranger, and that was to be expected. They hadn't, however, actually done anything to him. If the roles had been reversed, he knew, and a group of monitors had come across a lone Wild – Freelander – the outcome would be different.

"Yes," he said. "I w-was running away." He told Moses of being exiled to the outside in lieu of execution for the sin of spilling water on the Chairman. "It wasn't even my fault, but they would have killed me for it."

"Now, Hiroshi," Moses said, turning and looking down at Hiroshi. "You see why what we plan is necessary? What kind of society behaves in that manner towards it people? If they're that callous with the ones assigned to protect society, they must be even more heartless and uncaring toward those on the bottom rungs."

Hiroshi nodded. "I see, you're right," he said. "I think I've seen it all along, but meeting Leland here just confirmed it for me. New Liberty is a corrupt society that is a danger to itself and everyone around it."

"Worse," Leland said. "The current leader is insane. He is planning something terrible. I don't know what, but when I served on his security detail, I saw him having meetings often with Citizen Halifax, a scientist, and with the minister of defense, Citizen Wainwright. I was never close enough to hear what they talked about, but the looks on their faces when they spoke with him made me believe that whatever he plans to do, it scares them."

"Do you know if involves Freeland?"

Moses asked him.

The young monitor closed his eyes in concentration. When he opened them, he had a haunted look. “Once, he was talking with Citizen Halifax, and I just happened to wander near without them noticing me. I heard him say something like, ‘once you complete your project, I can begin to spread our influence beyond the fence.’ I moved away quickly, so I heard no more, but I believe he intends to invade your territory.”

Moses again stroked his beard. He looked at Hiroshi with a determined expression. “Now, do you see why we must do something, youngster?”

“Yes,” Hiroshi said simply. “And, we probably don’t have much time.”

Leland-27 looked from Hiroshi to Moses. “What about me?” he asked. “I can’t go back, but I guess you have no real reason to trust me in your community.”

He looked crestfallen, standing there in their midst, his shoulders slumped in resignation, looking down at the ground.

Moses put a beefy hand on the young ex-monitor’s shoulder, squeezing gently.

“Oh, I think we can find a place for you,” he said. “Welcome to Freeland.”

# 26.

Back in Freeland settlement, Leland-27 was given clothing to replace what was left of his monitor uniform. Moses had taken his flechette pistol, telling him that such weapons weren't needed in the settlement. He'd been assigned a cabin near the one Hiroshi shared with Clementine.

Moses had asked Hiroshi to introduce him to Freeland, so after changing into his new clothes, he joined Hiroshi and Clementine in their cabin.

The three of them were sitting around the small table in the center of what Rebecca Stennis called a parlor, sipping tea that the old woman had taught Clementine how to make from the flowers growing in the little plot in back of the house. Hiroshi had washed and changed in to clean clothing, and except for the stinging in his shoulder where he'd snagged himself on the wire, felt like a new person. The look of welcome on Clementine's face when he walked through the door, and the way she rushed into his arms, unmindful of how dirty and bedraggled he was, had contributed to his sense of wellbeing.

"Why did you lie and tell them I'd helped you?" Leland asked. "If I'd known at the time who you really were, I'm not sure I wouldn't have taken you into custody, or even shot you, and you must know that. Why would you want to help me?"

Hiroshi took a sip of the fragrant tea, looking over the rim of the cup, first at Clementine and then at Leland, who had already stopped using the number after his name, and was waiting for Abraham and Sarah to come up with a suggestion for an appropriate surname.

"It's hard to explain," Hiroshi said. "When you didn't shoot me right away, I had a feeling that you were different, I guess. You looked lost and afraid, and I remember how I felt when Clementine and I first ran away from New Liberty. Like you said, it just didn't seem right not to help someone who was lost. And, frankly, while you might have arrested me, I don't think you have it in you to shoot an unarmed person."

Leland's cheeks turned red and he looked down at the table top.

"You're probably right," he said. "Well, I'm glad I didn't shoot you. I guess I can never go back to New Liberty, and it's good to have someone here I can talk to, you know."

Hiroshi didn't say that he wasn't sure they'd have anything in common to talk about, so he changed the subject to the way Freeland was governed, which Leland found fascinating, particularly the fact that people could select their own occupation instead of having some faceless bureaucracy decide it for them before they were even old enough to make the decision for themselves.

"Have you ever thought about being anything other than a monitor?" Hiroshi asked.

"I hadn't until I was assigned to external patrol. I'd never been outside the fence before. In fact, I'd only ever been in the prole community once before, back during training. Except for worrying about being attacked by Wild Ones, it was nice being in a place where you couldn't see the air you were breathing. I think I'd like being a hunter or a farmer, you know, some occupation where I could be outdoors."

"Just think what the world would be like if everyone could live like that," Hiroshi said.

“Sure, it would be nice, but what can we do about it other than help anyone who runs away?”

Moses had, in a private conversation with Hiroshi just before assigning him to guide Leland around the community, left it to his discretion about sharing information about Freeland’s plans. There was little danger, since Leland didn’t know the terrain well enough to get back to warn New Liberty, and Moses would probably tell him at some point anyway, but he allowed Hiroshi the freedom of telling him earlier if he thought it wise. There was something about Leland that Hiroshi liked – nothing he could precisely identify – but, a feeling that he could be trusted. So, he told him of Freeland’s plans to try and incite a rebellion in New Liberty.

“I’ve already shown the proles that the monitors can be stood up to,” he said. “With the right fuse, Abraham believes we can ignite a rebellion.”

“But, these people here only have spears and arrows. How can they stand against the weapons the monitors have?” Leland asked.

“There are a lot more proles than monitors and citizens combined. If they all stand together, with Freelander help they could win.”

Leland shook his head.

“Maybe, but a lot of people would die in the process. One thing I remember from my monitor training is that you want to have some parity in weapons before going into battle against someone. To do otherwise is a foolish waste of forces and lives.”

“Some things are worth dying for,” Hiroshi said, and he realized that he meant it. “Besides, as long as the proles allow themselves to be treated as tools or animals, they’re as good as dead.”

Leland shook his head. “I don’t know. I think being alive, no matter the situation, is better than being dead. And, if the people here go against New Liberty, there’s no telling what Citizen Cruz and The Committee might do. I just don’t think arrows and spears are a match for the weapons the monitors have.”

“You’re saying that Freeland doesn’t stand a chance against New Liberty?” Clementine asked.

“No,” Leland said. “I’m saying that Freeland needs better weapons, and I have an idea on how to get them.”

# 27.

Leland's idea was ambitious – even audacious. He recommended a two-pronged attack on New Liberty, with one force hitting the fence east of the river to divert the monitors, while another went after the armory west of the river.

Many of the Freelanders posed objections, arguing that they were no match for the better-armed monitors. But after some debate, Moses decided that it was just audacious enough to have a chance of success. New Liberty, he reasoned, wouldn't expect people armed with only bows and spears to have the nerve to attack their fortified stronghold. If they hit hard, he argued, they just might succeed, and that would be better than waiting for New Liberty to attack them.

Leland had told them that he knew the

location of the monitor's armory where weapons and ammunition were stored. It was a concrete bunker near the west end of the northern bridge across the river, just inside the citizen's community. Because of its location, it was only lightly guarded. It was also in a wooded area, close to the river, and unguarded on that side. In none of his training, he told them, had a defense of the armory been discussed, the reasoning being that no one knew of its existence. All of New Liberty's defenses were concentrated on guarding the fence.

Hiroshi remembered from one of the map books in the book cache an old route to the area from the southwest that stayed south of the river. He assumed the fence would be as vulnerable where it entered the water on the west side of the river as it was on the east. Moses agreed, and added that because the previous incursions had occurred east of the river, no one would be paying any special attention to the area to the west.

It was decided that the raid would be conducted by a force of fifty Freelanders, including Hiroshi and Leland, and they would launch immediately, assuming that the New Liberty officials wouldn't be expecting them to return so soon. Another fifty Freelanders would make a feint attack on the fence east of the river to draw attention away from their move toward the armory. On the night before they departed, Moses gave Leland his new name – Freeman – an appropriate surname which the former monitor wore proudly.

Just before departure, Moses pulled Hiroshi aside. "I want you to stay close to Leland," he said. "And, I want the both of you to stay where I can see you."

"I can understand that you don't trust Leland yet," Hiroshi said indignantly. "But, don't you trust me?"

"Of course I trust you, son, but I almost lost you the last time, and I don't want that happening again. Until we have enough people who've learned enough from the books we brought back, you're Freeland's library. We can't afford to lose that brain of yours."

Hiroshi laughed as the older man patted him affectionately on the shoulder.

The two groups set out, and after passing through the northern checkpoint, Hiroshi's group turned southeast and followed a narrow, winding trail down the slope until they reached flat land.

Their path was generally southeast by east, across the flat plain that stretched from the foothills of the Appalachian Mountains to the coast, which now, with the rise in sea levels, was twenty miles west of its original position. The Atlantic Ocean and the

Chesapeake Bay had merged, wiping out the small fishing towns along the coast and mostly submerging cities like Norfolk, Virginia and Ocean City, Maryland, making them uninhabitable. With major metropolitan areas like New York City, Philadelphia, and most of the cities of New Jersey emptied of population, the smaller satellite towns and communities also ceased to be viable habitats since they depended on the large cities for power and other utilities. The rivers running through Baltimore and Washington, DC had risen, but not enough to cause flight. Cut off from the rest of the east coast, the two areas merged into New Liberty.

The plains, once home to wealthy suburbs, vineyards, and horse farms, was now a steamy jungle of derelict communities reclaimed by nature, vast forests of oak, maple, chestnut, beech, and black gum trees, competing with invading species of semi-tropical plants whose spores had been blown north by the wind, and hundreds of streams and creeks that crisscrossed the terrain.

The distance from Freeland to New Liberty by this route was about three-quarters less than the hillier northern route, but the boggy earth, oppressive heat and humidity, and biting bugs that tormented a traveler's every step, made it seem an eternity. By the time they reached an open area where Hiroshi knew they needed to turn north to get to the river, his face was a mass of bumps and pricks from the bites of mosquitos the size of dragon flies and dragon flies the size of fruit bats.

It was still an hour before sunset when they reached the river. Moses called a halt in a stand of trees a hundred yards south of the river. Hiroshi, Leland and the others flopped down wherever they stood, mentally and physically exhausted from the day's journey.

Moses walked over and knelt next to where Hiroshi lay on his back, his eyes half closed.

"We'll wait until dark and then cross into New Liberty," he said. "Looks to be at least two hours until it's dark enough, so everyone should be rested."

"I hope we're not going back the same way," Hiroshi said. "I'd really hate to cross terrain like that in the dark. I thought the mosquitos would eat me alive."

Moses chuckled. "Yeah, if you think the insects are bad in the daytime, you should see the size of the bats that come out at night."

# 28.

## *The Culling Ground*

The culling was scheduled for the hour before sundown. Factory and farm shifts that usually ended well after sundown were ended early so that the proles working them could be herded to the culling ground around the tall monument well before those selected for culling were brought out.

Proles dressed in their shabby brown singlesuits, many stained dark from their labor, stood around in sullen groups, their gazes steadfastly on the ground in front of their feet. Behind them, black-clad monitors, hands on their flechette pistols, stood in a single file. With their visors down, the setting sun reflecting off the surfaces made them look like ornately carved black lamp posts.

Washington Benedict stood in a knot of Columbus Height Crèche residents in the middle of the crowd on the north side of the ground. Through gaps in the crowd, he could just glimpse the hard packed earth that circled the stone monolith. Some of the smaller children pushed in close trying to get a look. Washington wanted to look away, but didn't for fear he would draw attention to himself. He was just tall enough and old enough to be eligible for the cleanup crew that the monitors always selected after a culling – those tasked with removing the ashes of the unfortunates chosen for culling.

He looked up at the top of the monument. The red lights, which normally were unblinking, were wavering, beginning to bathe the ground below in their crimson glow. What few on the ground knew was that the red lights were part of an air and missile defense system that had been installed in the monument in 2020 to protect the capital from attack. When things went south, the militia group that had taken control of the city had repositioned the laser-based system to protect against ground attacks. The weapon was capable of emitting an intense wave of heat to destroy attacking planes or missiles, and when employed against ground targets, was able to incinerate anything up to and including a main battle tank in a matter of seconds. It had been turned to use in executions during the tenure of Robert Cruz, at the advice of his religious advisors. Their reasoning was that it was an efficient, quick, and humane method, and the resultant ashes of the condemned could be used as fertilizer in the community's crop production. Forcing the prole community to witness the executions was Cruz's idea – he viewed it as an effective way to keep people under control.

The device in the monument was operated from a terminal in the basement of The Committee's headquarters, the former Pentagon, through what remained of the former capital city's wireless communications system. Wires connected the terminal to a parabolic dish on the building's roof which sent a signal to another dish located in the top chamber of the monument. The same dish system also carried the propaganda messages from the Ministry of Population Control to relays in the prole community, which forwarded them to the system of loudspeakers located throughout.

A murmuring sound, all the quiet conversations taking place, echoed throughout the area. As if a switch had been thrown, there was absolute quiet. The crowd on the west side of the monument parted. Two hundred proles, dressed in gray singlesuits, the attire of the condemned, walked through the space, flanked by ten monitors on each side.

Those in the crowd averted their gaze to avoid looking at the condemned ones as they shuffled slowly toward the base of the monument. When they were lined up in eight rows of twenty-five, facing the stone walls of the monument, the monitors withdrew and stationed themselves behind the crowd.

There was a crackle of static, and then a nasal voice came from the speakers placed around the area. "Residents of New Liberty," the voice echoed off the stone wall. "It is the duty of each to contribute to the welfare of the community. Those who violate the laws of the community, or who contribute nothing to the community through their labor, must be removed from that community. In this way, they will, as a final act, contribute to the future wellbeing of all."

The voice went silent to be replaced by a humming sound from high above. The red lights at the top of the monument began to pulse.

Washington Benedict lifted his head, looking first at the pulsing red circle high above, and then at the rows of people waiting numbly like so many cattle in the red aura of its glow. "Hiroshi," he said, quietly at first, but as those nearest him picked it up, louder. "Hiroshi, Hiroshi, always remember, always remember, Hiroshi, Hiroshi."

The chanting spread, slowly at first, but soon picked up speed like flames on dray grass, until every prole around the monument, including the condemned, was repeating it.

"Hiroshi, Hiroshi, always remember, always remember, Hiroshi, Hiroshi."

At the rear of the crowd, the monitors shifted nervously, looking at each other. They had never experienced this before. There was no precedent for it. In the past, the crowd had merely stood and watched dumbly as the event proceeded to its conclusion, and then shuffled back to their hovels.

In the basement room across the river, Hector Cruz stood behind the terminal operator. From the speaker on the wall above the terminal, the chanting came, faintly at first, then louder. "Hiroshi, Hiroshi, always remember, always remember, Hiroshi, Hiroshi."

He stared up at the speaker. His flesh felt cold, and his hands trembled.

"Do it, now," he snarled at the operator. "Get it over with."

"The machine has to get to maximum power," the young woman at the controls said. "It will be at least a minute more."

Cruz was shaking all over now. The

operator thought it was from anger, but it was from an emotion that was new to the Chairman – fear.

"I. Want. It. Done. Now!" Cruz said. "That is an order."

"B-but, citizen," she said. "If I activate it before it reaches maximum power, disintegration will not be instantaneous." Her protocols were exacting. The culling procedure was not to be torture. To activate early would result in death for the condemned, but rather than instant oblivion, they would be burned to death more slowly.

"I don't give a damn," Cruz said adamantly. "If you do not activate immediately, I promise you that you'll be in the next group of culls."

*"Protocol be damned,"* the young woman thought. *"He's insane, but he's in charge."* She reached over to a red button in the center of the panel and stabbed it.

The chanting was disrupted by the sound of screams, first of surprise, and then of agony. Fortunately, the device was almost at maximum, and was able to achieve total disintegration of the unfortunate victims within thirty seconds, but the young operator knew that they had suffered half a minute of absolute agony before being turned to small piles of gray ash, and even from several miles away across the river, thought she could smell the odor of seared flesh, clothing, and hair.

# 29.

When darkness fell, Moses ordered the group forward to the point where the fence descended the banks into the river. He accompanied Hiroshi down the muddy slope. As Hiroshi had anticipated, where the wires were submerged, they were rusty and weak. It was a matter of minutes to break enough to make an opening large enough for two men abreast to pass through.

Hiroshi went through first, followed by Leland. “You two wait for me,” Moses said, as he did a head count of the other men as they went through the opening.

Once Leland got his bearings, he took the lead, working his way along the river until the blocky concrete building the housed the armory was in sight. He stopped on a small rise, behind a clump of bushes, looking down at the front of the structure. There was one thoroughly bored-looking black-uniformed guard standing in front of the massive metal door.

"How do we get into that thing?" Moses asked.

Leland shook his head. "I'm not sure," he said. "I've never seen a guard outside before. Usually there's only two inside, and it's never locked. I mean, after all, there's no real threat over here. No citizen ever comes to this area, and the proles can't cross the bridge unless they're escorted by monitors."

"Damn," Moses said. "We can't have come all this way for nothing."

"Maybe he's just outside getting fresh air," one of the men said.

"Have you taken a deep breath lately?" Leland asked. "No one here in New Liberty goes outside unless it's absolutely necessary."

Moses laughed. "You got a point there, son," he said. "Okay, first thing is we have to take out the guard. Then, we'll just see where we go from there."

Leland shrugged. Moses rose slowly and began working his way toward the building. Leland and the others followed single file. About ten meters from the structure, Moses dropped to one knee behind a small bush and took his bow from his shoulder. He fitted an arrow and took careful aim.

There was a ‘twang’ and the feathered shaft zipped from the bow, flying in a shallow arc toward the unsuspecting guard. Before Hiroshi could even register the flight of the arrow, the monitor slapped at his neck from which the missile protruded. The man sagged against the wall and slid slowly down it to come to rest in a sitting position, his legs splayed out in front of him.

Leland looked appreciatively at Moses. “That was good shooting,” he said. “You must teach me to use a bow like that.”

They waited a few minutes, but there was no movement below them.

“Okay,” Moses said. “Let’s move up, but keep quiet.”

With Moses in the lead, the group filed slowly down the slope to the corner of the concrete building. The dead monitor, sitting in a dark pool of congealed blood, sat silently as if asleep. Moses stepped over the body to the door. He laid a hand on the cold metal and gave it a slight push. It moved quietly inward. He put a finger to his lips.

Putting a hand on the edge of the door, he eased it open far enough to enable him to slip through. He found himself in a narrow hallway that went forward to a lighted rectangle. He opened the door the rest of the way and motioned the others into the hallway, again putting a finger to his lips.

As Moses and Hiroshi came to the end of the hall, they saw the two monitors. The men were sitting at a small table in the center of a large room, the walls of which were lined with shelves on two sides and crates stacked to the ceiling at the far side. The shelves contained boxes, crates, and folded black fabric. The two monitors were absorbed in a card game and didn't notice that they had company, until the one facing the door happened to look up. His hand darted downward toward the flechette pistol at his waist, but Moses brought the bow up, an arrow at the ready and let fly. The shaft buried itself in the monitor's shoulder. He screamed in pain. The other monitor, seeing the arrow protruding from his partner's shoulder, started turning, going for his own weapon. But, when he finished turning, he found himself facing the ten men who had crowded into the room, five of whom had wicked looking arrows aimed at him. The sound of his partner's moaning, and the sight of so many sharp points aimed at his midsection caused him to reevaluate his intentions. He let the weapon drop to the floor.

"Now, that was a really wise idea, son,"

Moses said, moving forward to retrieve the two weapons. He motioned two of the men over. “Tie this young fellow up and stash him over there and after you get the arrow out of the other one and bind his wound, tie him up as well. The rest of you start grabbing as many of these weapons and ammunition as you can carry.”

Hiroshi walked to one of the shelves and picked up one of the folded cloths. “I’d take a few of these as well,” he said, opening a monitor’s uniform. “And some helmets.”

Moses stopped and stared at Hiroshi – then, he laughed.

“By dang, you’re right. That will come in handy. You’re getting pretty smart at this tactics stuff, youngster.”

# 30.

A group of sleepy looking men gathered around a round conference table in The Committee's headquarters just as dawn was breaking.

Sitting in his customary place, Hector Cruz looked haggard, with dark circles under his eyes and the shadow of fuzz on his haggard cheeks indicating that he had neither slept nor shaved. Sitting across from him, Gravius-One looked little better. His eyes were bloodshot, and the muscles in his broad, dark cheeks twitched continuously.

All of The Committee's main members, except for Nigel Halifax, were present, looking curious and concerned at being summoned at such an early hour.

Drake Edison looked from Cruz to Gravius. The worried looks on their faces caused the level of acid in his stomach to rise to the level of pain. He clenched his jaws to keep from belching, causing tears to spring up in his eyes. He didn't know what was going on, but he knew it was bad.

Hector Cruz looked around the table. All but Gravius avoided his gaze. That, he thought, was as usual. The monitor commander was the only one who would challenge him directly in this manner. He was also the only one who probably understood the significance of the previous day's events.

Cruz's gaze came back to Gravius, who still stared doggedly back. Finally, Cruz blinked and looked down at his hands which rested on the table. He felt a slight tremor from his wrist down. When he felt as if he might yawn, he breathed deeply and clasped his hands. *"That will keep them from shaking,"* he thought. *"I can't have Gravius think I'm afraid or worried."*

"I am concerned at the events of the past days," Cruz began slowly. "First, we have these two proles making a fool of two monitors and escaping." He fixed his gaze on Gravius, noticing the quiver in the man's cheeks. "Then, to add insult to injury, the prole, Hiroshi Jackson, comes back to New Liberty and escapes yet again, and we have indications that a group of Wild Ones came with him and actually entered the community. How is that possible, Citizen Gravius?"

"The boy seems to know the layout of the area well," Gravius said. "And, we only have a few monitors on patrol in the area at that time of night."

"As I understand it, had it not been for a prole reporting his presence to a monitor we might not have known he was even here.

Gravius nodded. Cruz turned his steely gaze upon Edison.

"That brings us to the unfortunate incident yesterday at the culling," Cruz said icily. "How do you explain that, Citizen Edison?"

"I d-don't understand, citizen," Edison said, not daring to look up from the table. "The culling went off without a problem. There was no incident."

Cruz's lips curled down in a sneer.

"What do you call the chanting?" His tone was scathing. "The crowd - even those selected for culling - was chanting that prole's name. That is an act of rebellion, and it cannot be tolerated."

Edison shrank lower in his chair. The chanting incident had worried him, but the crowd had dispersed peacefully, and he'd tried to put it out of his mind. He'd made a note to speak with his staff about maybe tuning up the orientation messages – he refused to use the term propaganda – to reinforce docility in the proles. He should have known, though, that Cruz wouldn't miss it.

"It *was* unprecedented behavior, but it didn't go beyond chanting," he said. "I believe a slight change in the messages we deliver to them will erase that impulse."

"You put too much faith in your propaganda messages," Cruz said derisively. "I think it's time for a stronger message to our worker population."

Before he could explain, a monitor slipped quietly into the room and walked over to Gravius-One. When the commander nodded, the monitor leaned over and whispered something in his ear, and then stood back to attention. Gravius's dark face creased in worry. He dismissed the monitor with a wave and turned to face Cruz.

"I'm afraid, citizen, that the chanting incident is not the worst of our problems," he said levelly. "Last night, someone attacked the armory, killing one guard and seriously wounding another. They took a large quantity of arms and ammunition."

Cruz's face drained of color. His mouth opened in shock.

"Who? How?" he demanded.

"The surviving monitors said it was a large group armed with bows and spears. They were dressed like the Wild Ones."

"How did a group of barbarians get inside the fence undetected?"

Gravius's face was ashen, and the quivering of his cheek muscles caused the flesh on his face to ripple.

"They were led by a former monitor, Leland-27, and the prole, Hiroshi Jackson," he said quietly.

"A monitor?' Cruz's eyes widened. "Wait, is that the one you exiled to the external patrol, the one who was supposedly lost in the search for Jackson?" Gravius nodded. "So, we now have a rogue monitor *and* a prole aiding our enemies.

Cruz looked across at Armand Wainwright.

"It would appear that your fears were well-founded, citizen. Sending the entire militia force away and leaving internal security in the hands of the monitors was not wise."

# 31.

Wainwright glanced at Gravius. He found himself enjoying the man's discomfort. For over a year now, since Cruz had made the stupid decision to send the militia force south to scout the former American military bases that dotted the south of the old United States in search of arms and ammunition, and to map out any potential military rivals that might spring up, Gravius and his monitors had been given complete control of the community's security.

A former general in the defunct American army, Wainwright had deeply resented being displaced by a glorified security guard. In time, he had come to hate the man with a passion. The monitors, in his opinion, were well-suited to perform internal security, and keep the proles in line, but it was his elite militia that was capable of securing the community's borders. Typical of Cruz, he thought, to come to that conclusion only after a crisis. The man wasn't capable of real strategic thinking, unlike his father, who Wainwright had respected.

"Unfortunately, citizen," he said. "We must now make do with what we have."

Cruz looked at him with a narrow-eyed expression that he couldn't read.

"The militia should be on its way back by now, surely," he said. "They can then take charge of our external security."

Wainwright didn't miss the way Gravius's lips turned down at that. As much, though, as he enjoyed the man's discomfort, he had to face the situation as it was.

"The last scouts indicated that the force made it as far as the new coast of what was once Florida," he said. "All of the military bases between here and there were completely looted before being deserted. They've not encountered anything more than a few scattered settlements hanging on by their fingernails -nothing to fear from any of them. They've started back this way, but without motorized transport, they're at least six months away from arriving." He didn't add that the militia commander had destroyed every settlement he'd encountered, slaying every man, woman, and child. He'd save that bit of information for later.

"That's not good enough," Cruz said. There was a note of petulance in his voice that Wainwright found irritating. "The Wild Ones have infiltrated New Liberty at least twice, and now they have weapons and traitors helping them. I'm leaving it to *you* to find an answer."

Wainwright saw an opportunity to finally put Gravius in his place, and at the same time, elevate his own status.

"Well," he said. "There's always the possibility of turning command of the external monitors over to me. After all, I not only have experience in combat command, but I'm far more familiar with conditions beyond the borders."

He didn't have to say, 'more familiar than my esteemed and hated colleague, Gravius,' but he could tell from the flicker of hatred he got from the man that his meaning wasn't lost on him.

Cruz smiled. *"Good work, Wainwright,"* he thought. *"You've just given me what I need to start bringing Gravius down."* He nodded at Wainwright. "That sounds like an excellent idea."

Gravius cleared his throat and leaned forward. "I'm not so sure, citizen," he said in his gravelly voice. “Disrupting the unity of command is not a good idea.”

“It would only be command over those doing external patrol,” Wainwright insisted. “I have no desire or need to worry myself over manning internal guard posts. I’m sure *you* are capable of that.”

The dig hit home. Gravius’s nostrils flared.

“We are more than mere guards,” he said.

“Oh yes, I forgot, you also babysit the proles to keep them in line. You can keep that, too, as far as I’m concerned.”

His massive fists clenched, Gravius started to rise from his chair.

“That will be enough,” Cruz said in a loud and commanding voice. “I have made up my mind. Citizen Wainwright will assume command of the external forces. You, Gravius, will maintain control of those inside the community. This is to take effect immediately. Now, Citizen Gravius, I have another task for you.”

“Yes, citizen, what is it?”

“The proles of New Liberty need to be taught a lesson that they cannot learn from information broadcasts,” Cruz said. “They need to learn that insurrection will *not* be tolerated. Therefore, I want you to take a unit of monitors into the prole community and deliver a lesson they will not forget."

Gravius stared across the table. *"The fool's losing his mind,"* he thought. *"That's the last thing we should be doing now. It'll only drive them to further resistance."* He knew, though, from the stony expression on Cruz's face that trying to dissuade him would not only be futile, but foolish. It wouldn't take much for the insane fool to order Wainwright to replace him entirely, or worse.

"Very well, citizen," he said. "I would request, however, that Citizen Wainwright be directed to provide assistance should we encounter any resistance from the proles."

That was as close as he dared come to stating that he thought the idea was bad. Under the table he crossed his fingers in hopes that Cruz wouldn't interpret his remark for what it really was. He knew from the expression on Wainwright's pale face, though, that he knew.

The defense minister lifted his eyebrows slightly. *"Smart move,"* he thought. *"It won't save your ass completely when Cruz decides to get rid of you, but it might buy you some time."*

"With Citizen Cruz's approval," he said. "I'll have a unit of the external monitors standing by to assist – should it prove necessary."

## 32.

Ordinarily, Gravius liked being right. In the present instance, however, it was decidedly unpleasant to be proved right in his assessment of the situation.

He'd gone straight from the early morning meeting to the monitor barracks at the bridge nearest Committee headquarters. He'd ordered up a team of twenty monitors, fully armed, and accompanied them across the bridge. He would personally command them, hoping that he would be able to keep events from spiraling out of control.

The officer in charge asked him what he was planning, and got a glacial stare in response. Gravius didn't tell the men what he wanted them to do until they arrived at the first prole residential building. As he predicted, there was no response to his orders other than, 'yes sir.' The monitors were trained well. They were conditioned to follow orders, and this they would do. Gravius, though, felt sick inside. Not that he had any special sympathy for proles, but he hated doing foolish things, and this, in his view, was just about the most foolish thing Hector Cruz had ever come up with, ranking right up there with sending the entire external security force off on a wild goose chase.

He pointed to five monitors sitting in the back of the truck. When they dismounted, he had them line up.

"You are to enter," he said. "And kill two people on each floor, no more, no less. Do you understand?"

One of the men raised a hand. Gravius nodded.

"What if we encounter resistance?"

Everyone knew the story of the two monitors who'd been killed at Hiroshi's crèche. Before, such a thing would have been unthinkable, but no longer. This worried Gravius. Never before had monitors had doubts like this. If this man's concern was shared by the others, they were in for trouble. *"The situation is worsening,"* he thought. *"Before the first shot is fired. Oh well, in for a penny, in for a pound. Maybe we can still salvage this mess."* He only wished that he really believed that.

"If anyone resists, do what is necessary," Gravius said.

As the five men entered the building, Gravius returned to the truck and ordered the driver to Columbus Heights. What he'd been ordered to do there was really gut wrenching. Killing adult proles, as wasteful as it was, only bothered him because it *was* wasteful, but children, even prole children – it offended his sense of right. His mission, as he saw it, was to maintain order. But, even docile proles were unlikely to remain so if wantonly attacked, and this was just that.

Cruz, however, had been specific. He wanted *everyone*, prole and attendant, at the facility eliminated. For some reason, he was convinced that the place was the center of the resistance he was sensing, and that the only way he could quash that resistance was to utterly destroy its center. "Cut off the head, and the beast will die," he'd said to Gravius just as he was departing. Gravius was convinced the man had finally gone completely insane, but was in no position to really do anything about it. So, for now, he would merely carry out the orders he'd been given to the best of his ability, and try to salvage it afterwards, if there was anything left to salvage.

The five monitors he'd sent into the building would complete their mission and move on to the next task on their list. They, at least, wouldn't have the distasteful task of killing children.

What Gravius didn't know was that when the monitors began shooting on the ground floor, information about what was happening moved to the upper floors like the speed of light. A middle-aged prole, on his way home after a late shift at the power plant, saw the truckload of monitors on their way to the Columbus Heights Crèche, and figured they were up to no good. He immediately turned and ran back into the alley.

By the time the monitors arrived at the crèche, all but five or six students, two attendants, and a prole janitor had slipped out the back of the building, and were running through alleys, led by Washington Benedict, who had been just about to depart for his work assignment, and was the first to get word that something was terribly amiss in the community.

In the meantime, the five monitors who had been left at the first building, after encountering no resistance on the first floor, were met with a deluge of furniture and crockery as they mounted the stairs to the second floor. With more than a hundred people occupying each floor, the ten story building had more than a thousand angry people who were unprepared to see their friends and relatives arbitrarily slaughtered. With almost a hundred angry proles behind them, and an unknown number on the floors above, they were soon pinned down in the stairwell, and fighting for their lives.

Unable to move upwards, they concentrated their fire on the targets below. Bloodied and torn bodies littered the stairwell and hallways, including two of the monitors, before they made their way back to the front exit and outside. The sound of hundreds of footsteps and angry yells was a greater motivator than anything else they'd ever encountered - the three surviving monitors began running, running for their lives.

At Columbus Heights, Gravius stood in the entry lobby, looking down at a couple of cowering attendants who were trying to quiet several brawling brats.

He approached one of the attendants, a skinny, red-haired female citizen with frightened blue eyes and a constellation of freckles on her pallid cheeks. "Where are the other attendants?" he asked.

The quaking girl shrank from him.

"I d-don't know," she said. Tears welled from her eyes. "A m-man came in, and t-then, they started l-leaving. He s-said s-something about k-killing. I d-don't know where they went."

The child, a young boy of about five, whose hands she'd been holding, buried his face against her thigh and began wailing.

"Shut that brat up," he ordered.

The attendant tried to soothe the frightened child to no avail. His crying had affected the others who also began crying.

Gravius looked around, disgust creasing his dark face. The monitors were shifting nervously from foot to foot awaiting his orders. From what he'd told the five he'd left in the residential zone, he knew they could guess what they were to do. *"But, orders be damned, I will not slaughter babies."*

"All right, monitors," he barked. "Outside and start looking for the trail of those who fled the facility. When you find them, you know what to do."

Fifteen pairs of boots slammed together in unison. The monitors whirled on their heels and fairly flew from the facility. Gravius stood there for a few moments longer taking in the scene around him. He had a sinking feeling in his massive chest.

# 33.

Ten blocks west of the crèche, Washington Benedict, Octavia Olympus, and fifty proles, ranging in age from ten to seventeen, huddled in a dust-covered first floor room of an abandoned apartment building.

"What do we do now?" a frightened looking boy with lank brown hair that hung over his eyes asked.

Washington frowned down at him. He was trying to come to terms with the fact that the others looked to him for leadership.

"I bet Hiroshi would know what to do," a girl cowering in the corner said. "He knew just about everything."

Washington felt a stab of jealousy, which was quickly replaced by guilt. They were right. Hiroshi *did* seem to know a lot of things that were far beyond the others' ability to imagine. Maybe, he thought, that was because he'd been raised differently, and had experienced so many things they never had. Maybe that's why Clementine preferred Hiroshi to him, and maybe that had been why he'd betrayed his friend to the monitors.

He'd been thinking of Hiroshi when he began chanting at the culling. It hadn't been planned – the words had come unbidden – but, once it started, and others picked it up, it just *seemed* the right thing to do, the thing that Hiroshi would have wanted him to do. It didn't completely make up for his betrayal, but it was better than nothing.

As he thought of his friend, Washington remembered how the two of them, when they were little, shortly after Hiroshi had been brought to the crèche, would play in the abandoned tunnels that Hiroshi had told him underground trains called subways had rushed through. Though partially blocked in places, the tunnels, Hiroshi had said, ran all over New Liberty, in some places near the surface, in others deep underground. They even ran underneath the river separating the prole community from the area inhabited by the citizens. Entrances to the tunnels were all over the community, often overgrown with tangled vines or covered by debris, they were avoided by everyone. If they could make it into the tunnels, even if the monitors came looking for them, there were so many side tunnels, they could hide forever.

"If Hiroshi was here," he said. "He'd tell us to hide in the tunnels."

"What tunnels?" the girl asked.

He told them. "It's dark down there," he said. "But, we can make torches. Hiroshi and I used to play there when we were little. If we go in far enough, no one will find us."

Washington knew that being in the dark wouldn't bother them. Because the output of the power plant was routed primarily to the citizens, they had spent most nights of their lives in darkness. The rats might be a problem, he thought, but they could learn to live with them. Anyway, it beat being torn to bits by a monitor's flechette pistol.

"We'll wait here until dark," Washington said. "I think there's an entrance to the tunnels not far from here."

Olympus had been standing in a far corner, silently regarding the young prole that she'd not noticed much before, quietly establish leadership of this group of frightened youngsters. What she'd seen with Hiroshi, and now with Washington, was challenging everything she'd been taught about proles. And, if it was true that the monitors were roaming through the community killing people, what she'd been taught about citizens was also in question.

She now walked over to where Washington squatted among the others. "I think it might be better if I returned to the crèche to look after the younger children left there," she said to him.

His expression as he looked up at her was troubled.

"That's not a good idea, headmaster. They're going to know we're missing, and since you weren't there, they might think you had something to do with it. Besides, someone needs to stay with this group and take care of them."

She smiled at him – the first time he remembered her ever doing that.

"You're doing a very good job at that, Mr. Benedict."

'Yes, but once I have everyone hidden in the tunnels, I'll have to leave." At the gasps of surprise coming from everyone, he held up his hands. "Not for good. I'll just be going to find Hiroshi to get him and his friends to help us."

## 34.

Hiroshi, along with Leland and two other Freelanders, had been assigned to scout the area east of the river to look out for possible New Liberty patrols. After their successful raid on the armory, Moses thought it likely that New Liberty might mount a retaliatory strike of some kind.

The five Freelanders had lain on the ridge line for nearly two days, watching the forested valley below, and had seen nothing but the occasional herd of grazing deer.

"You know," Leland said. "I don't think they're going to attack us. The militia was sent south over a year ago, and they're the only ones in New Liberty that know anything about the outside world. The monitors had never been outside the fence before the militia left, and it was only when they told us to look for you that a monitor got out of sight of the fence."

Hiroshi scanned the terrain once more, nodding. "I think you're probably right," he said. "But, Freeland hasn't survived this long by taking chances. If they don't attack, we'll have spent a few days camping here. But, if they do attack, we could be the difference between survival and extinction for our home."

Leland nodded. It was funny, Hiroshi thought. Both of them – well, three, counting Clementine – now thought of Freeland as home. Even stranger, he was beginning to think of Leland as a friend, and the feeling seemed to be mutual. Just a short time before, they were enemies. He recalled a quote from one of the books his father loved reading, an English translation of Chinese philosophy, 'circumstances change with the passage of time.' In this case, there had been a sea change in circumstances in a very brief span of time, and he felt that it was only the beginning.

The pressure of Leland's hand on his shoulder yanked him from his reverie.

"There's something in the bushes over to the southeast," he said quietly.

"Probably just a deer grazing," Hiroshi said.

"I don't think so. A deer would be moving the lower foliage, wouldn't it? Whatever is disturbing it now is about man-high."

Hiroshi tensed. While he had a phenomenal memory, recalling long passages he'd read years before, he was no match for Leland when it came to reading physical signs. The young monitor could see small details at great distances, and despite having been raised in the quasi-urban environment of New Liberty, quickly adapted his senses to the forests and mountains. If he thought it was a person moving through the brush, it more than likely was.

The other Freelanders, taking their cue from Hiroshi, also tensed, arrows nocked in their bows.

A figure emerged from the brush. The small herd of deer that had been grazing at the edge of the forest spooked and, leaping high in the air, fled to the north. Three bows were raised.

"Wait," Hiroshi said in a harsh whisper. "It looks like a prole."

"It is," Leland said. "His singlesuit is dirty and torn, but he moves like a prole."

"He's moving this way," Hiroshi said. "Let's wait until he gets closer."

As the figure neared, though, something

about the way it moved triggered a memory in Hiroshi's mind. The swing of the shoulders, and the way the feet splayed outward – it couldn't be, he thought. But, when the bedraggled figure was just over two hundred yards away, there was no doubt in his mind. Hiroshi stood.

"Wash," he shouted. "Wash, over here!"

Washington Benedict stopped, and looked around confusedly. His mind, he thought, must be playing tricks on him. He was convinced he had heard Hiroshi's voice, but out here in the wilderness that was impossible. When he finally saw the figure standing on the ridge above him, his heart leapt. It *was* Hiroshi. He stumbled forward. Tears streamed down his brown cheeks.

Hiroshi ran forward. Washington stumbled into his arms.

"Hirosh," he mumbled. "You're alive, you're really alive."

"Sure I am, Wash. But, what are you doing out here?"

Washington told his friend what was happening back in New Liberty, or as much as he knew of it.

"The monitors are killing people, Hirosh," he said. "For no reason, they're just killing people. We got as many out of the crèche as we could – the headmaster came with us. I hid them in one of the tunnels we used to play in, and came looking for you. She said you'd survived. I wasn't sure I believed her, but she seemed so certain, I had to look for you. I don't know what to do. I don't understand why they're killing people, Hirosh. Why?"

Hiroshi felt as if someone had dropped a large rock on his chest. He knew why the monitors were killing people – it was because of him. If he'd gone meekly to his doom rather than resisting; and killing; the monitors who had come for him, this might not be happening.

## 35.

Gravius hadn't realized that by ordering the monitors back onto the streets he was unlocking the gates to hell.

Once outside the building, the troop encountered the monitors fleeing from the first building, and got a garbled account of what had happened. This resulted in a disaster. In the next block, they encountered four proles who hadn't heard about what was happening, and who were on their way to work. When loudly challenged by the monitors they reacted the way most people would react when faced by a large crowd of armed, angry people – they ran. When they turned and ran, the monitors did what most adrenalin-fueled, angry, armed people will do – they opened fire. The four unlucky factory workers were torn to bloody shreds, and their remains spread over the sidewalk, parts of the street, and the wall of the building next to which they were when the darts struck.

This unfortunate incident was observed by the proprietor of the small shop on the ground floor of the building, who made the mistake of coming outside to see what was going on. When the monitors turned their weapons his way, he ducked back inside, ran through the shop and out the back, screaming at the top of his lungs, thus alerting the other residents of the block.

Frightened, confused, and not a little angry, proles began barricading themselves inside the nearest buildings. Those who sought shelter in the few one-story buildings on the block were quickly routed and killed. The lucky ones who had made it into multi-story structures quickly realized that the ground floors were little more than kill zones, and made their way to the floors above, blocking stairwells with furniture and empty crates. From the upper floors, at a range where the flechette pistols were of only minimal effectiveness, they began bombarding the monitors on the sidewalks below with whatever they could lift or throw, and in some cases that included objects of sufficient weight to disable any hapless monitor who failed to get out of the way quickly enough.

By the time Gravius had exited the

crèche, and reached the scene of the standoff, five of his monitors were sprawled on the sidewalk, their bodies mixed in with proles, while the remainder had sought shelter behind piles of trash and broken furniture, occasionally sending a fusillade of darts arcing up at open windows. A futile gesture at best, and each time met with a fresh avalanche of furniture and trash.

Gravius stopped just outside the drop area and called for the senior monitor in charge of the group. A black-clad figure moved from behind a pile of tatty stuffed chairs and ran zigzagging toward him.

"Yes, citizen," the man said as he reached Gravius.

"What the bloody hell is going on here?"

"We were carrying out our orders. The proles resisted. They are now barricaded inside the building out of range of our weapons."

*"Holy shit,"* Gravius thought. *"Who would ever thought the fucking proles had it in them to fight back. This is a total cluster fuck, and it's landed right in my lap. Surgical elimination of a few proles to break any resistance, my ass. We have a full-scale war on our hands now, and there's nothing left to do but try my best to win it."*

"Very well, monitor," he said to the waiting man. "You're in charge of this position. Send me one man to act as a runner. I'll send for reinforcements."

The monitor nodded and ran back to comply. As he waited for the runner, Gravius composed the messages he planned to send – one to Wainwright asking for reinforcements from among the external patrols, another to his executive across the river directing him to send all remaining monitors to the prole community, and a final message to Cruz informing him that his plans to send a message to the proles about resistance had achieved just that.

However it ended, Gravius knew that his career was over. There was no way that Cruz would accept responsibility for the mess he'd created. He would be lucky, he thought, to escape with his life. More than likely he'd be assigned, no consigned, to some desk job in the bowels of the headquarters building, keeping track of crop yields or citizen births, kicked off The Committee and forgotten.

# 36.

## ***Freeland***

“We have to do something,” Hiroshi said. He was shaking, and almost in tears.

He, Leland, and Washington were sitting in Abraham Moses’s living room. The big man had listened to Washington’s story, and was now thoughtfully stroking his beard.

“I reckon you’re right, son,” Moses said. “But, what can we do? The New Liberty forces outnumber us, and even with the weapons we took from the armory, they still outgun us. I’m not sure we’re ready yet to take them on.”

Hiroshi sank down in his chair. His frustration was mounting, along with his feelings of guilt.

Leland timidly raised a hand. Moses

smiled and nodded at him.

"It seems to me," he said. "If Washington and the others from the crèche ran away, it's likely that others did as well."

"Makes sense," Moses said. "But, how does it help us?"

"Well . . . with the militia away, the monitors are responsible for all the security in both communities. Any kind of resistance from the proles would generate fear across the river like you can't even imagine. When I was in training, the instructors talked more about the danger of a prole rebellion than an invasion from outside. I imagine that all security right now is focused on the prole community."

Moses' lips turned up and his eyes took on an impish twinkle.

"Son, are you saying what I think you're saying?"

"If we go back in the way we went to attack the armory, we'd be coming in behind most of the security. We could attack the headquarters, which is only lightly guarded at the best of times. If they're focusing on troubles in the prole community, it'll be even more lightly guarded, because just about everyone will be trying to handle that problem."

"What would happen if at the same time a small force attacked the fence east of the river?" Hiroshi asked.

Leland laughed. "They'd probably shit their pants," he said. He looked over at Washington. "I take it some of the proles are fighting back?" Washington glowered at him, but nodded. "Think about it – the monitors are up to their asses in angry proles – two more enemies appearing from two different directions will confuse them like you wouldn't believe. Our tactical training was only about how to deal with unruly proles. The militia was supposed to protect the border."

Moses ran his fingers through his beard, looking from one young man to the other. He was deep in thought, assessing the pros and cons of an attack on New Liberty.

"You know, the two of you together come up with some pretty good ideas. This just might work," he said. "So, let's talk about how we go about doing it."

The three of them came up with a plan that was bold – in Moses' words, as audacious as their raid on the armory, because it would be a repeat of that raid.

First, Leland would spend a day teaching a hundred Freelanders how to use the weapons stolen from the armory. A hundred flechette pistols, if employed at the right time, could help redress the imbalance in arms between the two sides. Fifty Freelanders, armed with the pistols, would go with a force of two hundred to attack the fence east of the river, while fifty others would be part of a group of a hundred who would mount an assault on the citizen's area. Leland came up with the idea of dressing twenty-five in monitor uniforms. With this group leading, it might be possible, he reckoned, to get deep within the area before the attack was detected. Moses, accompanied by Washington, would lead the force in the east. He gave Hiroshi command of the second force, and Hiroshi asked that Leland be made his second in command. There was a bit of grumbling among some of the older Freelanders, but Moses reminded them that, despite their youth, Hiroshi and Leland were the most knowledgeable of the area in which they'd be operating, so it made sense. Under his stern glare and no nonsense tone of voice, the grumbling subsided.

The two forces were primed and ready to march on the third day. Their sendoff was somber. Clementine stood with Sarah Moses, a forlorn look on her face. The older woman had a stoic look that mirrored that of her husband. Hiroshi tried to look brave and stoic, but as he looked over his shoulder and saw Clementine with her head against the other woman's shoulder, he felt like crying himself.

# 37.

Gravius was fuming as he walked toward the door to The Committee's main meeting room. That Cruz would summon him back across the river at the very time that his forces were beginning to make a little headway against the barricaded proles made no sense. A few more hours and they would clean out the main centers of resistance. That should cause the rest to capitulate, but even if they didn't, it would just be matter of time.

He was angrier when he entered the room and found Armand Wainwright sitting at Cruz's right hand, a smug look on his face.

"Come in, citizen," Cruz said with a smarmier note than usual in his voice. "Have a seat, please."

He was tempted to stand, but decided that it would be a childish gesture, so he took the seat opposite Cruz. “Why did you need to see me, citizen?” he asked. “I was busy with the situation across the river, and really should be there with my men. We almost have it under control.”

“Ah, yes. The situation in the prole community. Very disturbing to say the least. That is, in fact, precisely why I called you here.”

“I understand that you might want an update on the situation,” Gravius said. “Most of the proles remain holed up in three buildings near the central district, but we should have them out by the end of the day.”

Wainwright made a quiet snickering sound. Gravius glared across the table at him.

“Well, citizen,” Cruz said in a cold voice. “I appreciate your efforts in that regard, but really, this should never have happened in the first place.”

*“That is for damn sure,”* Gravius thought wryly. *“And, if you’d listened to me and not ordered this fool’s mission, it wouldn’t have happened.”* He wanted nothing more than to utter the thought aloud and then follow it by smashing his fist into the idiot’s face. Instead, though, he took a deep breath and locked gazes with Cruz. “You’re right, citizen,” he said evenly. “It shouldn’t have

happened. But, we are bringing it under control."

"I'm greatly disappointed in you, Citizen Gravius. I expected better of you. Now, I must make an important decision, one that is very difficult."

"You wouldn't be thinking of calling for a withdrawal, would you? While I didn't think the operation was wise, now that we're committed, pulling back would send the wrong signal to the proles." Gravius knew that to terminate the operation before routing the rebellious proles would lead to open season on his monitors. He'd have to send them into the prole community in platoon strength to maintain any semblance of order.

He should have known better, though. Cruz had no intention of ending the operation.

"No," Cruz said. "I not only want the operation to continue, but I want *every* prole in those buildings terminated as well. No, I'm afraid, Citizen Gravius, that your performance in this situation has left much to be desired."

Gravius felt his cheeks burning. He'd been a monitor before this punk was born, and had been commander of the monitors since he was a teenager waiting for his father to die. "*What* about my performance fails to satisfy you, citizen?"

"I'm not sure I like your tone."

"I don't think Citizen Gravius meant any disrespect, citizen," Wainwright offered. There was no sympathy or sincerity in his voice. "Perhaps some details about the shortcomings we discussed would be in order."

Gravius leaned forward, his clenched fists on the table. He was dangerously close to losing it. "Shortcomings? What shortcomings? Everything was done according to regulations and protocol. There was no way we could have anticipated prole resistance. In fact, if we hadn't gone in with such force and begun killing them – *per* your orders, I might add – they might have calmed down on their own."

"I should think," Wainwright said in an oily tone. "That the chanting the day of the culling should have been a warning that something was amiss, and that prole boy killing two of your monitors was a blatant act of rebellion. I, for one, *don't* think they would have calmed down."

Of course he'd been aware of those incidents. That was why he'd argued against Cruz's idiotic idea of punishing the community. It would have been far better to let things cool down. Cruz's stony expression, however, made it clear that he wouldn't hear any criticism of his decision, nor would he accept any blame or responsibility for the outcome.

"Very well," he said. "I accept responsibility for what went wrong."

"How noble of you," Cruz said. His voice dripped with sarcasm. "I'm afraid, though, that's not enough. Citizen Gravius, I am hereby relieving you of all duty, and placing you under house arrest until The Committee can decide on the appropriate punishment."

Gravius stood. "With all due respect, citizen," he said. "You can't leave the monitors without a commander while they're in the middle of a battle. They're capable, but they need direction in a crisis like this."

"I'm not leaving them leaderless, citizen. Citizen Wainwright will assume command of the monitors effective immediately."

That told Gravius all he needed to know. Wainwright had probably even talked Cruz into the damn mission in the first place, knowing it would fail. *"I knew the son of a bitch hated my guts, but I never thought he wanted my fucking job as well, or that he'd risk the entire community in order to get it."*

"As you wish, citizen," he said. He removed his flechette pistol and laid it carefully on the table. "I will be in my quarters." *"And, I hope the two of you rot in hell."*

He turned slowly and with his back straight walked out of the room.

# 38.

The two Freelander forces separated after reaching the river. Hiroshi's group headed due south, following close to the river bank, while Moses led the other group across the river and turned south paralleling the other force on the east bank. At times the two groups could see each other.

Moses kept the boy Washington Benedict close at his side. The kid was completely lost in the wild, making as much noise as a wounded elk and tripping over every root, limb or rock in the trail.

"Listen up, son," he said to Washington as they approached the last rise before the border fence. "When we get to the top of that rise yonder, I want you to find a place to hide and wait until I send someone for you."

Washington looked at the older man, a

puzzled look on his dark face. "Why? I should be with you to show you the best places to go," he said.

"Once we're past the fence, you will. But, there's going to be a lot of shooting making that happen, and I don't want you to get hurt, so just do as I say." *"Besides, with you making so much noise, the shooting might start before I want it to."*

They found a flat spot bordered by thick bushes at the lip of the ledge leading down toward the fence which could be seen in the distance. Moses stayed on the ridge for a long time, observing the fence. Something about the scene worried him – there were only six monitors guarding the gate, and for the past two hundred yards they hadn't noticed any signs of patrols. It seemed too easy. Nothing, he knew, was ever handed to you on a platter.

An accomplished hunter, Moses decided to do a little flushing. He pulled one of the men clad in a monitor uniform aside, and then divided the remaining force in half. He sent one group to the right and the other to the left.

"Now, son, here's what I want you to do," he told the man he'd kept behind. "Just go stumbling out of the bushes like someone's chasing you, and head straight for the gate."

The man smiled, pulled down his helmet visor and turned toward the fence. He was no more than twenty yards from the sentries, when what had looked like innocent bushes were flipped aside and ten more monitors rose, all with their weapons aimed at the oncoming man. Suddenly, though, the monitors found themselves staring at a variety of weapons on their flanks, including flechette pistols held by figures dressed in monitor uniforms. As brave and well-trained as they were, this was a situation that had never been addressed in any of their training or experience, so they did what prudent people do under such circumstances – they dropped their weapons and raised their hands.

Moses had them disrobed, trussed and stashed in the pits they'd been hiding in, and left two of his men to guard the gate. With Washington guiding them, the Freelander force began its trek toward the center of New Liberty.

"Stay alert," Moses said. "If you see anyone with a weapon, use your judgment, but don't shoot at unarmed people."

Having won their first engagement without firing a shot, the men were energized. Several pumped their fists in the air. Even young Benedict seemed pumped up, after seeing a large group of the dreaded monitors so easily defeated.

Moses, on the other hand, walked along with a sober look on his face. *"This must be what it was like long ago, when young men marched off to battle, so full of energy and bravado. I hope they're all alive at the end of this day to celebrate a full victory, but Lord knows, I can't guarantee it.*

## 39.

Armand Wainwright rode across the bridge nearest the scene of the fighting between the monitors and the proles. The black uniform he'd had in his quarters for months – from the time he'd decided he wanted Gravius's job – fit him perfectly. He sat in the front seat with the driver, his back erect, like the warrior he pictured himself to be.

His plans were working perfectly. It had been child's play to convince Cruz to take punitive action against the proles after the chanting incident, which the little popinjay took as a personal insult. Prole resistance had been fortuitous. His original plan had been to claim that Gravius had overreacted and killed more proles than necessary, which would negatively impact on production quotas. The fool's inability to complete the mission quickly was perfect. It hadn't taken much prodding to make Cruz believe the former monitor commander was incompetent. *"My first plan was a masterpiece, but this is just as good,"* he thought smugly. *"There's always a plan B."*

As the vehicle neared the fighting, he could hear the rumble of voices, punctuated with the occasional burping sound of a flechette pistol. Rounding a corner, he saw a group of monitors behind piles of discarded furniture, facing a four-story building from which the occasional object was thrown to crash down on the sidewalk near them. A monitor would fire a volley of darts at the building, only to see them bounce ineffectually off the brick walls.

Wainwright gruffly ordered the driver to stop the vehicle. He got out and stomped up to the men.

"What the hell do you men think you're doing?" he demanded.

A broad shouldered, tall monitor turned from the barricade and stared down at him. He knew the man was a citizen, and wondered what he was doing here wearing a monitor uniform without helmet and visor. "Who the fuck wants to know?"

Wainwright pulled himself up to his full

height, six inches shorter than the man he faced, and puffed out his chest.

"Your new commander wants to know," he said icily. "And, unless you want to be summarily executed for insubordination, you'll answer my question."

"Uh . . . sorry . . . commander," the man said. "We're . . . trying . . . to . . . get . . . the . . . proles . . . out . . . of . . . the . . . building." The man hadn't been told that Gravius was no longer commander, but no one would make such a claim if it wasn't true. He took a deep breath to steady his trembling. "They're holed up on the second and third floors, and have managed to get three or four weapons off dead monitors. We'll have them out soon, though."

Wainwright looked around. On the sidewalk in front of the building, two monitors and five proles lay in grotesque positions. The door of the building hung askew on its hinges. He could see the edges of furniture piled against the door.

"You're not doing a very good job of getting them out," he said.

"They have the door blocked," the man said. "And, every time we try and assault it, they bombard us with stuff. I've already lost six men – the two whose bodies you see there, and four more inside."

Regarding the man disdainfully, Wainwright was even more convinced that taking the monitors away from Gravius had been the right thing to do. The man was too soft, and it was reflected in the performance of the forces under him. Truly tough soldiers didn't pull back because of the fear of taking casualties. If his militia wasn't off on Cruz's fool mission, it would have stormed the building long before now, ignoring casualties, and killed everyone inside. Gravius's troops were little more than glorified security guards. Well, he'd quickly change that. This mission would cull the weak, and he'd whip the survivors into a force almost as good as the militia.

"So, you lose a man, and you pull back like a bunch of cowering girls? You're a miserable excuse for soldiers."

"We're not soldiers – we're monitors. Our job is to maintain order, not engage in combat."

Wainwright decided that an object lesson was in order. The monitors at the barricade had turned their attention away from the building and were watching his conversation with the individual who was no doubt the alpha of this pack. He walked up to the man, who stood stiffly at attention. "Give me your weapon," Wainwright ordered.

The man hesitated, but years of conditioning kicked in. He withdrew his flechette pistol and handed it to Wainwright.

"For cowardice in the face of the enemy," Wainwright said in a dry voice. "I hereby sentence you to death."

He lifted the pistol and pressed the trigger, sending a half dozen of the razor-sharp darts into the man's chest at close range. The monitor took two steps backward as the steel darts slammed into his chest, and then, with blood gushing from beneath his visor, sank lifeless to the pavement. Wainwright turned to the others.

"Now, is there anyone else who wants to see what I, your new commander, do to cowards?"

He stood before them, the weapon pointing at the ground, his free hand on his hip. The men looked from him to the crumpled body of their comrade, lying on his back in a spreading pool of blood. No one spoke.

"No? Good then," Wainwright said. "Now, here's what we're going to do. You will assault that building. You will ignore casualties – in war, some will die – and you will continue to press forward until you breach that front door. Once inside, you will move from floor to floor. You will eliminate all

– I repeat, *all* – enemy resistance. When that's done, we will move on to the next nest of rebels and repeat the operation. Is that clear?"

"Yes, commander!" they said in unison.

Wainwright smiled. He pointed to a small monitor in the middle of the pack of armed men. "You are in charge," he said. "I want this building cleared within the next three hours. Is that clear?"

"Yes, commander," the man said, darting his eyes nervously at his dead comrade.

# 40.

Hiroshi called a halt at the side of a street about five hundred yards from the armory.

"Why are we stopping?" One of the Freelanders asked.

"Listen," Hiroshi replied. There was a humming sound in the distance. "I hear a truck, and it seems to be moving this way. Get down, all of you, until we know what's happening."

While the rest of the group found suitable hiding places, Hiroshi and Leland stood at the side of the road. Soon, a cargo truck came around a corner, heading toward them, belching clouds of black smoke.

"Looks like just the driver and one man," Leland said. "Probably on the way to the armory for more ammunition. What do you plan to do?"

Hiroshi smiled and pulled his visor down. "That is our ride to the objective," he said simply.

Leland pulled his visor down as well and stood beside Hiroshi. The truck came to a halt as it reached them. The driver leaned out the window.

"What are you two doing here? Everyone's supposed to be over in the prole community," he asked.

"We came from the bridge," Hiroshi said, pointing toward the nearby bridge over the river. "Some proles were trying to assault our post, and we ran out of ammunition."

"Yeah, same thing across the river," the driver said. "Fucking proles are holed up in buildings, and we're expending darts at a fantastic rate trying to drive them out. The shit has truly hit the fan."

While Hiroshi talked to the driver, Leland walked nonchalantly around the front of the truck to the passenger side. The other monitor, watching his comrade talk to Hiroshi, hadn't noticed.

"I was wondering," Hiroshi said. "If you could give us a ride when we get our supplies?"

"Uh, I don't know. We've got this new commander now, and he's a mean ass. We were told to get supplies and get our asses back real ricky-tick, you know. You'll just have to walk, friend."

"That's too bad," Hiroshi said. He pulled his pistol and shot the driver in the face.

Temporarily blinded by the spray of blood and flesh as his partner's head exploded, the monitor on the passenger side didn't even have a chance to reach for his weapon before Leland sent six darts into his chest.

They pulled the corpses from the truck and stashed them in the bushes alongside the street. Hiroshi signaled for the others to come out.

"I wonder what he meant by having a new commander," Leland said.

"Maybe the guards at the armory will know," Hiroshi said. "Why don't we drive down and ask them."

# 41.

Gravius sat brooding in his sterile, undecorated apartment in a two-story white brick building not far from the headquarters. He was truly only Gravius now. With his dismissal from the position of commander of the Force of Social Monitoring, known as the monitors, he'd lost his numerical designation. Like all monitors, when he'd entered training, in his case at the age of twelve, his surname had been deleted from all records, and that had been so many years in the past he no longer remembered what it had been. His parents had died when he was an infant, and he'd been raised in a series of foster homes until the crèche system was introduced, and after that, he'd lived in crèches until being moved to the monitor training school. Monitors were seldom dismissed, forced to interact with other citizens who had surnames. He would be a marked man – all the more so because he'd been head of the monitors for so long, and because he was such a distinctive figure, with his broad shoulders, shaven head, and dark skin. The only fortunate thing, if anything about his situation could be called fortunate, was that Cruz was unlikely to allow him to live much longer.

It was just as well. While he could no longer remember his father's name, he did remember that he'd descended from a long line of law enforcement people, stretching back to the beginning of the twentieth century, when one of his forebears became one of the first black men to become a detective on the police force of the old District of Columbia. Being a cop was in his genes, and if he couldn't follow that profession, there was little left to live for. He regretted that the years had erased the names of those distinguished forebears from his mind.

His chief regret, though, was that he'd not resisted Cruz's stupid plan with more vehemence. Not that it would have swayed the rest of the spineless members of The Committee to his side, but that it might have caused Cruz to back down. That, he felt, had been his true failure, and because of it, many good monitors had died, even more proles had died needlessly, and the future of New Liberty, the community he'd sworn to serve and protect, was in jeopardy.

He had no personal affairs to put in order. He'd never married, nor in fact had he even had any long term liaisons with any of the female citizens who saw association with the head of monitors as a key to social status. He would not be mourned. His parents, whoever they had been, were long since dead. That was what life had become since The Apocalypse, you're born, you struggle, whether you're citizen or prole, and you die. And, when you die, your remains are recycled as fertilizer to grow food which is consumed by those coming behind you. He laughed softly. *"Hell, when we die, prole and citizen become equal at last, nothing more than a pile of gray ash to be turned under the earth. I wonder what the proles think about that."*

So lost was he in his thoughts, he didn't hear the door whisper open, and didn't become aware of the presence of another in the room with him until he heard a soft throat-clearing sound. He looked up to see Hector Cruz standing just inside the door, a strange expression on his face. He didn't bother standing. Under the circumstances he didn't think it would make much difference.

"What do you want . . . citizen?" he asked. He made no effort to mask the disdain in his voice.

The only response Cruz had to this deliberate insult was a minor upward twitching of his brows.

"I thought you'd be happy to know that Citizen Wainwright has been no more successful in putting down the prole revolt than you."

"So, another head for the chopping block." Gravius laughed mirthlessly.

"Oh no, citizen," Cruz said. "His end will be far more glorious than yours. They will sing his praises for generations, telling their children how he went out in a blaze of glory. Futile glory, but glory nonetheless." He laughed. There was, Gravius thought, a strange, maniacal note in that laugh.

Gravius looked up at the man who had once been his boss, someone he'd watched grow into manhood. Even as a child, though, he'd always worried Gravius. *"Now, I understand the meaning of the phrase, 'this child will be the death of me.'"* He laughed again. "I get no pleasure in another's misfortune," he said. "Even when he brought it upon himself. My one regret is that the community must pay for my mistake."

"Why should you care about the proles?"

"I *care* about New Liberty," Gravius said. "It is not just the proles who will suffer because of this misadventure of yours."

"Mine? How dare you impute that *I* am at

fault in this debacle. It was your failure to carry out my orders that brought us to this place."

Gravius wanted to argue, wanted to make the effort to show the fool how wrong he'd been. But, to what end? Cruz was as capable of seeing his own faults as the sun was of rising in the west.

"As you wish, citizen," Gravius said. "It really doesn't matter now, does it? Many will suffer needlessly for the mistakes that have been made."

"Maybe, Citizen Gravius, maybe, but you and I will, at least, be here to witness the glorious end. And, it will be glorious, of that you can be sure."

With that, Cruz spun on his heels and walked away. For many minutes after he'd gone, Gravius sat in silence, but his mind raced. He was angry, as angry as he could ever remember being, as he thought about how Cruz had used him and then so callously discarded him, as he was apparently now preparing to do to Wainwright. Then, the phrase 'blaze of glory' hit him like a thunderclap. He suddenly felt cold, as he realized what that phrase meant.

Cruz had gone beyond insane.

# 42.

Moses and his unit came up behind the position occupied by Wainwright and a small group of monitors. Washington had taken them to the subway tunnel where he left Octavia Olympus and the other children. Moses had left two of his men to safeguard them, and then instructed Washington to take him to the scene of the fighting.

The group was just starting around a corner when Washington grabbed Moses' arm. “Up ahead, monitors,” he whispered.

Moses quickly signaled the group to fall back.

“So,” Washington said. “What do we do now?”

“Why, we attack them, son. You wait here until the shooting's over, you hear.”

Washington nodded without hesitation.

Moses arranged his forces, two rows of ten of the men who were dressed in monitor uniform formed up shoulder to shoulder. Behind them, the rest of the force arranged themselves so they couldn't be seen from the front. He then gave the order to move out.

As they got closer, they could see that one member of the group wasn't wearing a helmet, and he seemed to be in charge. The group was so preoccupied with the proles throwing furniture at them from the building in front of them, Moses and his men were just outside the effective range of the flechette pistols before anyone noticed their presence.

Wainwright turned and saw the approaching monitors. He smiled.

"Ah, reinforcements have arrived," he said. "You men get up here and get ready. We're about to assault the building."

Moses called the group to a halt.

"Get ready," he said in a low voice that could only be heard as far as the second row, but that was far enough. Everyone tensed.

The monitors ahead of them began shifting nervously. One of them walked over to Wainwright. "Commander," he said. "I don't think those are monitors."

"Why? What makes you say that?"

"We don't move in tight formations like that unless we're dealing with a riot."

Suddenly, Wainwright felt a flash of panic. "You men, forget the proles for now. Turn and fire on that group!"

The monitors turned and fired a salvo of darts. The metal missiles arced out only to bounce harmlessly onto the pavement fifteen feet short of Moses and his men.

Moses laughed.

"Well, look at that. Guess these pretty little popguns have a few limitations," he said. "Front ranks, ready, kneel!"

The front two rows dropped to their knees. Behind them stood four rows of Freelander archers, each with bow at the ready. The front rank fired and knelt, followed by the next three in order. Bowstrings twanged. The arrows flew up in a low arc like a flight of slender, wingless birds. In seconds, they found their targets.

Wainwright opened his mouth to scream, but the sound was cut off by the arrow that pierced his throat, exiting the back of his neck. All that came out of his mouth was a great crimson gusher as he sank to the pavement. Half of the monitors also fell, mortally wounded, while the others had arrows in various parts of their anatomies, and lay writhing and screaming in pain.

That quickly, the battle was over. Unaccustomed as they were to prole resistance, they were even less prepared for an armed force that could reach out to them from a distance their flechette pistols couldn't reach. The monitors left alive dropped their weapons and raised their hands.

## 43.

At the armory, after overpowering and securing the sentries, Hiroshi and Leland learned of Gravius's dismissal.

"If that dickhead Wainwright is in charge," Leland said. "Things are going to go real bad, if they already haven't. Gravius at least cared about the people under him. That guy only cares about himself."

"Well, what do you suggest we do?" Hiroshi asked.

"We need to go and find Gravius. He'll know what to do."

Hiroshi took twenty men dressed as monitors in the truck, and with Leland driving they drove quickly across to the building where Gravius had his quarters. The other men were directed to proceed along the river to the first bridge and wait for further orders.

A monitor stood guard at the entrance to the building. Leland got out of the truck and approached the man.

"What are you doing here?" the guard asked.

"I was sent by the . . . new commander," Leland said. "He has something he wants me to ask Gravius."

"Give me the message, and I'll relay it. Citizen Gravius is under house arrest."

Leland squared his shoulders, lifted his visor and glared directly at the visored man. "I was told that the message was for Gravius's ears only," he said. "You know how the new commander is. He wouldn't like to hear that you stood in the way of me completing my mission."

"Shit," the man said. "I know what you mean. This new guy, Wainwright, is a complete ass. Okay, you can go in, but make it quick."

Leland slapped the man on the shoulder, smiling. So, he thought as he slipped through the door, Citizen Wainwright has moved in on Gravius. That might just make what he had to do easier. He knew his former commander had no love for Wainwright, who he regarded as an ass-kissing martinet.

He rapped lightly on the door.

Gravius's gravelly voice answered his knock. "Come in."

When Leland walked in, his visor up, Gravius's eyes widened in surprise. He rose and clapped a hand on the young man's shoulder. "So, you didn't die after all. Good to see you, son."

"Yes, I'm alive, commander, thanks to Hiroshi Jackson and his friends. I hear you're not doing so well these days?"

Gravius laughed. "I have had better days. So, you and the rebellious young prole have hooked up, eh? How did that come about?"

Leland gave him a quick recap of his adventures. "But, now, Hiroshi's people are being slaughtered, and I can't believe you'd think that was right, commander. We have to do something."

"I don't disagree with you, son," Gravius said. "But, as you can see, I'm no longer in charge. Wainwright's in charge of the forces across the river."

"Don't worry about him. We have forces taking care of him. But, we need to gain control of this side of the river. You could help us with that."

Gravius frowned. "You're asking me to become a traitor?"

"I'm *asking* you to help save our community. We're destroying ourselves. I know I was raised to think of proles as somehow less than human, just work units to be kept in line. Well, I've gotten a chance to know Hiroshi, and he's every bit as good as I am, in most ways, better."

The boy made a point. Gravius knew this. What's more, he knew that what Cruz was planning was even worse than what the monitors were doing. When he became a monitor, he *had* sworn to defend the community. Letting Cruz get away with what he planned would be a violation of his oath.

"Hell, son, when you're right, you're right," he said. "I knew saving your hide was a good idea. Okay, I'll help you invade New Liberty, but first, there's something we have to do over at headquarters."

Leland looked puzzled.

"I can't explain it yet, boy. Fact is, I hope to hell I'm wrong. But, if you can get me past my guard outside, we need to get a move on."

That was the easiest part. Leland just walked outside, put his flechette pistol to the guard's head and marched him outside to the truck where Hiroshi and the others waited.

They tied the hapless man up and tossed him into the back of the truck among the Freelanders.

# 44.

In the control room in the basement of the headquarters building, Hector Cruz paced behind the chair in which sat the nervous-looking young redhead. As she fidgeted with the controls on the board before her, she glanced anxiously over her shoulder.

She wanted to tell him to sit down and stop distracting her, but she knew he had a reputation for throwing tantrums – and other things, so she just gritted her teeth and tried to focus on the knobs, dials and screens in front of her – an almost impossible task as he paced so close she could smell the scent of the soap he'd used to shower and feel the heat of his body through her blue tunic.

“How much longer will you be?” Cruz asked petulantly. “You've been fiddling with those controls forever.”

"I'm sorry, citizen," the harassed young woman said. "I've widened the aperture as you directed, but that means the device will take much longer to get to full power. The change in diameter of the circle of coverage takes a much larger charge to get the same output, and the circuits can only take so much power. I can't make it go any faster without burning out the circuits."

Except for a few technicians who lived and worked in the building, and of course, the Committee, no one knew the full capacity of the culling device. Some technician, during Cruz's father's tenure as Chairman, had discovered that the laser could be refocused, with a radius that encompassed all of the populated area of New Liberty, and with some boosting, could still deliver lethal rays. It couldn't be focused very specifically at first, but Cruz had driven the technicians to work on focusing it in circles of different radii, radiating out from the center. What he had the technician doing now was creating a circle that took in some eighty-five percent of the prole community, or to the east bank of the river and out toward the perimeter, stopping just short of the power plant and most of the factories. Once the power reached maximum, the device would incinerate everything within the circle, buildings and humans would be reduced to ash. His security chiefs couldn't end the prole rebellion, but he, Hector Cruz, would end it, and no one would dare challenge him ever again.

The military-funded scientists had developed the weapon around 2020, when they finally discovered a way to effectively direct the heat that develops when a laser weapon is activated. The combined gas-electrical process, and new focusing methods, gave them a weapon that could either fry the guidance components of an incoming missile, or incinerate an attacking jet – and its pilot - instantaneously. When the technicians who worked for Cruz's father learned how to re-aim the device toward the ground rather than the air, the practice of culling was born, but not put into real practice until after the old man's death and his son's elevation to the chairmanship. It was seen at first as a more humane method of execution because of its speed. But, the impact of the public executions on the population quickly turned it into a tool for maintaining control over the workers. Now, Cruz would bring it to its ultimate purpose – it would be his ticket to eventual control of what was left of the world.

He fumed down at the back of the girl for a few seconds. He didn't understand the technology behind the weapon, and resented having to depend upon those he considered inferior for its use. If he could get his hands on the hidden books, though, he could learn.

He knew he could, because he knew he was smarter than any of the others. He would allow a select few to share part of his knowledge, but would retain the bulk for himself, and with Nigel Halifax's project, he would be around to enjoy this new power for a long, long time.

As he thought of the scientist, he walked to a table in the rear of the room, and picked up the phone. He dialed the extension to Halifax's lab.

"Yes, citizen," the plummy voice answered. Halifax knew who was calling. No one else ever called him.

"Have you solved the final problems with the process?" Cruz asked.

"I believe I have, citizen."

Cruz smiled and looked up at the ceiling. *"At last,"* he thought. To Halifax he said, "And, you've taken the necessary steps to ensure that only you know about this?"

"I . . . have," Halifax's voice trailed off.

"I know that you were attached to your assistants," Cruz said without a trace of sympathy. "But, this process in the wrong hands could be very dangerous. It had to be done."

"I . . . suppose . . . so, citizen. But, it . . .

will take me a long time to train new assistants." *"And, an even longer time to get over what you've made me do."*

"Don't you worry about that," Cruz said. "I'll take care of it."

Cruz broke the connection, and walked to the door. He pushed it open and stepped outside. The monitor standing sentry duty at the door to the control room snapped to attention.

"I have a special job for you," Cruz said. "And, it must be done immediately."

## 45.

Hiroshi and Leland, with an unarmed Gravius walking between them, and fifteen Freelanders in monitor uniform following, approached the main entrance of the headquarters. Two monitors stood guard on either side of the large double doors. They came to attention as the group approached.

Before the sentries could challenge them, Leland stepped forward. “We have orders to bring the traitor to Citizen Cruz,” he said.

Whether it was the tone of authority in Leland’s voice, or the look of abject surrender that Gravius affected as he stood there with his head bowed, the guard was convinced. He saluted and stepped aside.

The group swept into the large entrance lobby. Except for a few bored looking citizens sitting behind counters at the left, the lobby was empty. In front of them was a large bank of stairs, formerly escalators, but their motors had long since frozen, leading up to the upper levels of the building. Around to both side of the stairs were large archways leading to the many intersecting corridors. They took the right side, and a short way down the hallway, Gravius pointed to an unmarked door.

"That leads down to the control room," he said. "I'm sure we'll find Cruz there."

"I can't believe he's really planning what you think he is," Hiroshi said.

On the walk from his residence to headquarters, Gravius had told them of his suspicion that Cruz planned to target the culling device against the larger prole community.

"I don't know if it's technically possible," Gravius said. "But, I do know that Cruz is perfectly capable of doing it. I've always suspected that his father's *accidental* drowning in his bath wasn't really an accident. You two are too young to remember, but it was after he became Chairman that even citizens were required to give their children to a crèche for rearing. I guess he wanted to make sure there wouldn't be a son around to do to him what he did to his father. I hope I'm wrong, but my gut tells me I'm right."

Hiroshi shook his head. "He sounds as if he's insane," he said.

"The line between genius and insanity is thin, young man,' Gravius said. "When things first started to fall apart, a few people got together and did what they could to try and hold it together. They had to make some rough decisions, but initially, it was for the right reasons. Over time, though, those in charge grew to like being in charge, and out of that emerged people like Hector Cruz. Growing up, he had everything, but it was never enough. Yes, I suppose he *is* insane, but then, the rest of us stood by and allowed him to do what he has done, so I guess that makes us insane as well, doesn't it?"

# 46.

Nigel Halifax looked up as the monitor entered his office without knocking. The black-clad figure, his visor reflecting the light of the lamp on Halifax's desk, looked like some huge insect.

"What are you doing here, monitor?" he demanded.

"The Chairman sent me to get the notes of your research," the muffled voice said.

Halifax stood. "Very well, let's go see him," he said.

The monitor drew his pistol, and aimed it at Halifax's chest.

"No, not you, just your notes."

"That's impossible," he said. "I must be there for him to understand the notes."

"He does not think your presence will be necessary," the monitor said, and squeezed the trigger.

Six steel darts bored into the scientist's chest. He felt an immense pain as he fell back against his desk. Then, the pain was replaced by a creeping, cold feeling that seemed to start in his legs and flow upwards.

His vision was dimming, and the approaching monitor looked like a figure in thick fog. He was having trouble breathing.

"Why?" he asked weakly. The metallic taste of blood was in his mouth. "Why did he order you to do this?"

"It doesn't matter, citizen," the monitor said. "But, before you die, you will tell me where you keep your notes."

Halifax tried to laugh, but the pain in his chest made it impossible. All that came out of his mouth was a pitiful croaking sound. So, the Chairman was tying up *all* loose strings. After ordering him to kill his entire staff – and the sight of the writhing young men and women in the lab after he released the gas into the ventilation system brought tears to his eyes; the salty tears flowing down and mixing with the blood that was now leaking from his nostrils and from between his lips. Cruz intended to keep all knowledge of the new process to himself – to be in a position to dispense immortality to whom and when he chose.

"You don't understand," he said, gasping for air. "I am my notes. I burned all notebooks and papers after committing them to memory." *"Without me, Cruz has nothing."* And then, he did laugh. Despite the pain, he laughed. A fountain of blood gushed from his mouth, spattering the monitor's uniform, but Halifax continued laughing until his body jerked in a spasm, and went stiff. He slid slowly to the floor, his eyes glazing over. His last thought was, *"Fuck you, Citizen Cruz. I get the last laugh after all."*

The monitor shoved the body aside and began searching desperately for notes, a notebook or journal – anything that might pass for research material. The Chairman would be livid if he returned without them. They had to be in the office somewhere. He yanked out drawers, went through the pockets of the corpse's singlesuit, and looked in every nook and cranny, increasingly desperate as he found not a single word written upon a single sheet, no recording media – nothing.

When the late Nigel Halifax's office looked as if a small hurricane had swept through it, the monitor stood in the center of the room turning in a slow circle. He was in full panic mode. If he went back to Cruz to report failure, he'd be as dead as the pasty-faced scientist.

He backed slowly out the door. In the corridor he looked right and left. To the right was the way back to the control room, and his certain death. To the left the corridor, he knew, wound around the inner perimeter of the building, arriving at a large space that had once been a loading bay. It had large double doors to the outside world on the side of the building near the river. He turned left and began walking.

# 47.

When Cruz returned to the control room, he resumed his hovering over the beleaguered technician. The woman was sweating from the combination of the concentration required to balance the power input controls and the frustration of having him standing so close that she could feel the heat from his body.

"If the present rate continues," she said. "We should achieve full power in thirty minutes."

"I don't understand why this should take so long," he said, leaning forward.

The woman flinched as she felt his bony thigh against her shoulder.

"The radius of the circle is larger by a multiple of more than ten, citizen. But, in order to have a beam with sufficient power, it requires more than ten times the amount of energy. Building up to that level of energy must be done with care lest it cause an overload and explosion."

Cruz didn't understand what she was saying, and didn't want to understand. He only wanted the damn machine up and running. He pointed to a small screen. A red line moved slowly across the bottom from left to right. It was about halfway across. Above the line, a series of numbers blinked on LED insets. "Is that the power indicator?" he asked.

The technician nodded.

Cruz watched the glacial movement of the red line. His pulse thumped. He gave no thought to what would happen when the line reached its right terminus. That thousands would die in a blaze of intense pain, and hundreds of square blocks of the prole community would be reduced to ash, didn't cause him a moment of unease. He knew that a few would survive. Those currently working in the factories and fields and in the few residential structures that were outside the device's circle would survive. But, they would never forget the sight of the world around them going up in flames, of those who would dare oppose Hector Cruz being turned into grey ashes. And, from those ashes, Cruz would build a new world – his world – one that he would rule forever. In time, as he rebuilt the population of New Liberty, rebuilt a more compliant cadre of workers, technicians and soldiers, he would expand his control. He would share his secrets with few. Maybe a small inner circle of advisors who helped him rule. He might even select one or two to share Halifax's treatment. It would be good to have someone to keep him company over the coming centuries. He could always use the other little procedure he'd had Halifax develop, should anyone appear to be threatening his position.

It would be he, though, who would decide. He would hold the power of life and death over all. And, he thought, he'd start by eliminating useless people like the lump of a technician sitting in front of him.

"How much longer until it's ready?" he asked.

The woman sighed, which caused Cruz to fume inwardly. "Still about thirty minutes," she said.

The red line looked as if it hadn't moved. He pressed forward, willing it to increase its pace across to the right.

A scuffling sound from outside the room pulled his attention away from the technician. As he turned, the door slammed open and two monitors walked in. Then, his eyes widened as Gravius walked in behind the monitors.

"What are you doing here, citizen?" he demanded. "You are under house arrest."

"I'm here to keep you from making a bigger mistake than has already been made," Gravius said.

"You're too late. It has already been set in motion." He moved to block their view of the control panel. He had to stall for time. Clearly, Gravius had suborned the monitors set to guard him. But, if he could distract them long enough it wouldn't matter. And, once the monitor returned with Halifax's notes, his position would be secure. Maybe he would keep Gravius on longer. "Look, citizen," he said. "Perhaps I acted a bit hastily in your case. I'm putting you back in charge of the monitors. Maybe you could even replace that fool, Wainwright, and be in charge of all the community's defenses."

Gravius shook his head. "No, citizen," he said, his dark face contorted into an angry scowl. "It is you who are too late. Your reign of terror is over."

Beads of sweat popped out on Cruz's face. His eyes darted from side to side, as if looking for a place to run. "But, I'm doing what's best for the community, don't you understand. We must have order. And by reducing the population and instituting better control procedures, we can achieve that – perfect order. And, you and I could be in control of that."

"There is no such thing as perfect order," Gravius said. He took a step forward. "Your father understood that. He knew the system we'd put in place was unsustainable, that's why he was planning to make changes just before he died."

Cruz laughed. "Yes, my dear father," he said. "He was a weak man. He actually believed that he could create a society where everyone was equal. He was planning to grant full citizenship status to the proles and abolish the crèche system."

"Your father understood that people who have a stake in their community work harder than those who are compelled to work."

"My father understood *nothing.* He would have thrown away everything we worked for and built. There are better way to control workers, and I have them. Once we reduce the prole population to a manageable level, you'll see."

Gravius shook his head again. "You're talking about genocide. I can't let you do that."

Cruz stared at Gravius and the two monitors. His nostrils flared, and the veins on his neck stood out like cords of thick twine. "You can't stop me," he snarled. Spittle dribbled from his quivering lips. He whirled back toward the control panel, and grabbed the technician, yanking her from her chair and flinging her toward Gravius. While he might not understand the workings of the device, he'd been present at enough cullings to know how it was activated. He lunged for the red switch in the center of the panel and pulled it down. Then he twisted until the switch broke off in his hand A loud hum filled the room. The red line inched slowly toward the right. Cruz turned to face them, his eyes bulging and red. "Too late," he cried triumphantly. "It's too late."

Gravius moved forward and shoved him from the panel. "You damn fool," he shouted. "What have you done?"

"What none of you had the guts to do," Cruz said, smiling. "I've stopped the prole insurrection – stopped it in its tracks. And, I've ensured eventual development of the utopia we've always dreamed of. Citizens will thank me one day."

The humming grew louder.

Gravius turned to the young technician who was cowering at Hiroshi's feet. Her face was pale.

"Can this thing be stopped?" he asked her.

"No, not without the switch," she said in a quavering voice. "Once activated, it will continue to send signals to the device until it reaches full power, and then it will fire. There's not enough time to repair the switch."

Gravius spun and grabbed Cruz by his collar, shaking him as a terrier would shake a squirrel. "You fool. You're committing mass murder."

Cruz only laughed. A maniacal sound. He'd finally snapped. "Too late. Too late," he crooned. "Now, it's all mine. All mine at last."

Gravius had the look of a beaten man. "There's nothing we can do," he said, looking gravely at Hiroshi and Leland.

Hiroshi moved forward and lifted the technician by the shoulders. "You said this machine here is sending signals to the device, right?" The woman nodded numbly. "If that signal stops, what happens?"

"If the s-signal is interrupted," she said. "The device will continue to generate heat until it burns itself out – I think. I'm not sure, though."

Hiroshi had never seen the controls

before, but he remembered what he'd read about machines. If the master control signal stopped, the device would be left without instructions. It shouldn't be able to complete its cycle. *Shouldn't,* but he wasn't sure. He remembered something else his father had told him once, "When action is called for, act without hesitation. If things are going wrong, the wrong action won't make them any worse, and the right action just might be the first thing that pops into your mind." He drew the flechette pistol and aimed at the blinking lights on the panel. He pressed the firing stud, sending dozens of metal darts into the panel. When the first darts struck, it got an instant response.

The metal tips of several darts pierced the thin metal covering of the control panel, causing a short in the electrical circuit. Sparks flew in all directions, and the hum was replaced by first a sizzling sound, and then a high pitched whine. Smoke began pouring from the panel. The red line flickered and then the screen went dark.

Cruz, seeing the smoke and sparks, pulled away from Gravius and flung himself at the panel. "No-o-o-o-o!" he wailed. He grabbed the metal panel, which had thousands of volts coursing through it. His body bucked and began smoking. His face contorted and his tongue protruded from his mouth. Blood began streaming from his eyes and ears. His hair caught fire.

The whine grew louder.

"That can't be good," Leland said.

"I think we'd better get out of here," Hiroshi shouted.

He grabbed the technician and began shoving her toward the door. Leland and Gravius followed close behind. They just had time to make it through the door, slam it shut and get ten feet down the corridor, when there was a loud bang, and then silence. The door hung drunkenly from one hinge, partially opened. Thick gray smoke poured from the room, bringing the smell of burned plastic, flesh, clothing, and hair into the corridor.

"The controls are dead," the technician said. "I don't think the device can fire now."

"I hope you're right," Hiroshi said.

"Where did you get the idea to do that?" Gravius asked.

"Just something I remembered," he said.

They walked back up to the main floor and out of the building. As they walked around toward the river side, they could see the top of the monument. The red lights in the openings were flickering rapidly. Hiroshi thought he could see white smoke coming from the structure.

Suddenly, the structure was enveloped in a bright white light and billowing smoke. A few seconds later, a sound like a thunderclap reached them. As the smoke thinned, they could see that the top twenty feet of the structure was gone. The jagged stones were blackened, and a thin trail of smoke drifted up to join the smog from the factories.

Leland tapped Hiroshi's shoulder and pointed toward the river. A large group of people were heading toward the headquarters. As they neared, they could see a small, bedraggled group of monitors in front, their hands clasped above their heads. Following them were more monitors, accompanied by men carrying bows and spears. Hiroshi recognized Moses at the head of this group.

"Looks like our people won the day," he said. He turned to face Gravius.

"It looks like that indeed," Gravius said. "To whom do I surrender?"

# 48.

While the proles, under the watchful eyes of Moses' troops, began the job of removing the bodies and cleaning up the mess in their community, Moses, Hiroshi, and Leland met with Gravius in The Committee Room to discuss the terms of New Liberty's surrender.

"I guess you're the man in charge now," Moses said to Gravius.

"It would seem so. What are your terms, citizen?"

Moses chuckled. "I'm just Abraham Moses, Mr. Gravius," he said. "We're not much for titles in Freeland. Anyway, the only terms are that you folk here not take any offensive action against us. You're probably going to need some assistance getting things back in order. We're willing to help you there. We could also use some of the goods you produce in your factories, and we'd be willing to trade some of the things we grow for them. I reckon that's it. The rest is up to you."

"Trade is a good idea. And, you're right - we have to take responsibility for ourselves. There are a lot of changes we need to make. One of the first will be to appoint a new commander of the monitors." He turned to Leland. "You think you're up for the job, son?"

Leland's face was a study in confusion. "Uh, I don't know," he said. "Do *you* think I am?"

"If I didn't, I wouldn't have suggested it." Gravius chuckled.

"Okay, I'll do it."

"Good. From now on, you're Leland-One," the former monitor commander said.

"No," Leland said.

Gravius looked at him, his brows arched high. "What?"

"I," said Leland. "am Leland Freeman, not some anonymous drone with a number affixed to his name. And, I think the rest of the monitor force should also have surnames. We could have titles for job descriptions, like squad leader and such, and even ranks, but I think everyone should have his *own* personal identity."

Gravius regarded his former young subordinate through nearly closed lids for a few seconds. Then, he slapped his big hands on the table and laughed.

"You're absolutely right, Citizen Freeman," he said. "You're in command, and it's your decision to make. While we're talking about identities, I think the term monitor to describe our people leads to unfortunate connotations. I think we should change the name to New Liberty Police Force. What do you think of that?"

"I agree. Monitors are there to control people. Police serve and protect, and that's what we should do. I like it."

They discussed a few more things, such as ending the practice of monitors, now police officers, patrolling the streets with visors down, obscuring their faces, or going on routine patrols in large units, while Moses and Hiroshi looked on.

When Gravius and Leland were satisfied with the security situation, Gravius moved on to some more fundamental changes he thought were necessary for the survival of New Liberty. He started with abolishing the distinction between citizen and prole – every individual in New Liberty was a citizen. While he felt the fence should stay in place for a while, he decreed freedom of movement for all citizens of New Liberty, and unrestricted entry for Freelanders. The crèches would remain, but would be converted to boarding schools and care facilities. Their main missions would be providing education to all children as well as a place parents could leave children during the work day. Culling was, of course, abolished. Prisoners who couldn't be rehabilitated would be kept incarcerated. New Liberty no longer had the death penalty.

With the deaths of Cruz, Wainwright, and Halifax, there were vacancies on The Committee. After first changing the name to Advisory Group, Gravius decided that the former prole community should be represented on it.

"You seem like an intelligent lad," he said to Hiroshi. "I think you would be an ideal advisor."

"Thank you, but I'll be going home to Freeland," Hiroshi said. He looked at Moses who nodded slightly and smiled. "I know someone, though, who would be just as qualified – my friend, Washington Benedict."

"I think Hiroshi is correct," Moses said. "That young man impressed me as an effective leader who is respected by his community."

Gravius nodded. "Very well, then. I think we no longer need a ministry of population control, but Drake Edison is a decent enough person. I believe he would make a good minister of trade and agriculture." Everyone nodded. "I also think we need gender balance. After all, more than half the population is female. I was impressed with the young woman who ran your crèche, Mr. Jackson – Olympus was her name, was it not?"

"Yes," Hiroshi said. "Octavia Olympus. She was a tough headmaster, but she was always fair."

"Good, let's see how she functions as minister of education, health, and social welfare. Now, one final personnel change – I'll be dismissing the good Elder Robertson from the Advisory Group. I don't think it should concern itself with spiritual matters. That's what got us into this mess in the first place."

Moses smiled and stroked his beard. "I think you're off to a good start, Mr. Chairman."

Gravius nodded his thanks, but had a worried look on his face. "There is one other matter, Citi-, er, Mr. Moses," he said.

"What is it? And, please just call me Abraham."

"Wainwright's militia is expected to return in about six months. I'm not sure I can have the community's defenses set up to defend against them in that time-"

"-There's no need to worry," Moses said, cutting him off. "Freeland is prepared to assist in the defense of New Liberty, just as I assume you would come to our aid if needed."

The new leader of New Liberty smiled and sighed. He leaned across the table, extending his hand to Moses. "On that, my friend, you can rely."

"I will leave a small contingent here to help you in rebuilding what was destroyed," Moses said. "But, tomorrow, the rest of us will be returning to Freeland."

# 49.

The next morning, Gravius and his new Advisory Group were at the west gate to see Moses and his group off. There were handshakes and wishes of safe travels. Hiroshi had emotional farewells with Washington Benedict and Octavia Olympus, both of whom were still reeling from their new appointments.

Leland Freeman had an honor guard of police officers lining the path to the gate. As Hiroshi approached him, he held out his hand.

“Safe journey, friend Hiroshi,” he said. “And, thank you.”

“I did nothing,” Hiroshi said.

“You did more than you know, my friend. You gave me myself.”

The young police commander's eyes glistened. The two embraced, and after pulling back, shook hands.

"Be well, Leland," Hiroshi said. He turned and caught up with Moses at the head of the group of Freelanders.

"Next stop, home," Moses said as Hiroshi came alongside.

Hiroshi gazed toward the west. *Home.* It wasn't a concept that he'd thought much about before. He realized, though, that he'd never thought of New Liberty as home after being separated from his parents. Until he and Clementine ran into the arms of the Freelander patrol, he'd been floating in limbo like a dandelion spore in the breeze.

"Yes, home," he said quietly.

Moses cleared his throat. "I was wondering, Hiroshi. You never mentioned the books to Gravius or the others. Why was that?"

"I don't know. Maybe it was just habit. I kept the secret for so long I maybe just kept quiet as a reflex. Or, maybe I'm just not ready to completely trust them."

"Hm, you have a point," Moses said. "I think Gravius is an honorable man, and I feel sure we can trust young Leland. But, changing the direction of a society takes time.

They must learn to crawl before they walk, and the knowledge in those books would enable them to run. That could make them dangerous, not only to others, but to themselves. In the proper time, we can share with them."

Hiroshi nodded. There was wisdom in the older man's words. But, he was also reminded of something Moses had said, 'power corrupts.' That was the disease infecting Cruz. With his knowledge of where the books were hidden, he possessed a kind of power over others. Could he remain uncorrupted? *Always remember.* His father's words reassured him. As long as he remembered the dangers of being seduced by the possession of power, he should be able to stay on the proper course.

## 50.

Hiroshi awoke from the first sound, peaceful sleep he'd had for as long as he could remember.

The gray light of early dawn seeped through the gaps in the curtains.

They had arrived back in Freeland after the two-day journey from New Liberty, arrived to a hero's welcome. Sarah Moses had organized a large banquet. There was a long night of eating, drinking and dancing. Hiroshi remembered dancing with Clementine, Sarah, and several other Freeland women, and probably drinking more of Sarah's dandelion wine than was good for him, but, except for a slightly dry mouth, he felt no ill effects.

In fact, he felt warm – warmer than he should feel.

As he tried to turn in bed, he bumped against something warm and soft. As his eyes adjusted to the dim light, the warm and soft something resolved itself into Clementine, snuggled against his arm. He distinctly remembered going to bed alone after they returned from the banquet. Clementine had gone to her own room in the house they'd shared since their arrival in Freeland. But, here she was, nestled against him, her slender hands tucked beneath her chin.

Hiroshi felt the breath catch in his throat. He could hear his own heart beating.

Clementine's eyes fluttered open, and she looked up at him.

"Good morning," she said sleepily. "I hope you don't mind, but it got lonesome in my room, so I sneaked in here and crawled in next to you."

She lifted her shoulder, pulled one of his arms under her body, and rested her head in the junction of his neck and shoulder. Her hair tickled his nose.

Looking down at her, Hiroshi felt a strange sensation – unlike anything he'd ever felt before. Clementine moved her body against his. She then reached up and grasped his neck gently. Smiling, she began pulling his face toward hers.

At that moment, Hiroshi knew that he had finally found a home.

***The White Dragons.*** A novel of international intrigue by Charles Ray. Uhuru Press, North Potomac, MD, 2013.

## Critical acclaim for *The White Dragons*

'From the first few pages, this sinister mystery will have the reader wanting to know more . . . the eerie uneasiness and chilling sense of cruelty due to the desolate location and cut-throat atmosphere of KGB-like politics are palpable." *The Foreign Service Journal.*

Thursday, May 8, 1975, Washington, DC

Lesley Carter was worried.

First, she'd been held up by her boss, and feared she'd miss her bus. The L1 Metro bus arrived at the stop at Twenty-third and I Streets at 6: 40 pm, and was seldom late, nor did it wait long. If she'd missed it, she would have been looking at more than an hour wait for the next bus. She could take a cab for the 20-minute ride to her neighborhood, on Calvert Street, near the National Zoo, but didn't feel like paying the ten dollar fare.

She was breathing hard as she arrived at the already crowded corner, near Washington Circle, just north of George Washington University Hospital. She'd nearly run from the Department of State building's E Street side, fearing that her short legs wouldn't enable her to move fast enough. She found a clear spot near the front of the crowd and proceeded to pay her fellow commuters no mind; a small group that included several elderly black ladies in gray-green scrubs who worked at the hospital, a portly white businessman in a suit that was rumpled from his own walk in the humidity of mid-May in Washington, DC, three young men who looked like students from the university, and two girls in the plaid skirts and white blouses of a nearby private Catholic high school. She didn't notice the slender, narrow faced man with close set eyes and dark brown hair combed straight back from a high forehead, dressed in dark blue shirt and pants who had been behind her from the moment she crossed F Street, and who now took up a position at the rear of the crowd.

She was breathing hard from her walk, but a glance at the cheap Timex watch on her left wrist showed her that she'd made it with ten minutes to spare.

Despite not missing her bus, she still felt antsy. It had been a surreal day.

She was just settling into her first month on the job as desk officer for the tiny Central Asian country of Dagastan in the European Bureau of the Department of State. A grade 3 Foreign Service Officer, she was on her fourth tour, the first domestic assignment since finishing the orientation course and French language training seven years earlier. Getting the desk officer slot had been a surprise; she was a consular officer, and would normally been assigned to the Bureau of Consular Affairs upon return to the U.S., but, in her last posting, at the U.S. Embassy in Dakar, Senegal, she'd been assigned to the political section's most junior position with responsibility of reporting on activities among the country's ethnic minorities. She had so impressed the embassy's deputy chief of mission, he'd run interference to get her a coveted desk officer job, which would prepare her for more senior assignments outside the consular area; and, this was her dream.

A conscientious person; typical of her Wisconsin Protestant upbringing; she threw herself fully into the job, often working late into the evening, surpassing even some of the workaholics who routinely stayed in the office until past six to show how 'hard' they were working. In her case, she actually worked.

A detail oriented person, she often noticed the small things that others missed; thus, when she noticed a small item, only a few sentences really, in the intelligence digest prepared by the department's Bureau of Intelligence and Research, or INR, about the killing of two Dagastani government officials with the suggestion that foreign elements might have been involved, and then, after crosschecking, discovered that the embassy hadn't reported anything on it, she sprang into action. First, she drafted a cable to the embassy, for the political counselor, asking for any information the embassy had on the incident, and its assessment of the impact it would have on Dagastani politics. Not wanting to bother the office secretary, a sour faced civil servant who liked to remind the young desk officers that she worked for the country director, not them, she'd prepared the cable herself, requiring the typing on a cumbersome multi-copy form of ten green sheets with carbons interlaced, requiring that each sheet be dealt with to make corrections. For that reason, she kept the message short; tactful, but brief. It was when she'd taken it to James Whitman, the country director for that region that sat on the border between Europe and Asia, that her troubles began.

As soon as Whitman had finished reading, he put the paper on his desk, pushing it away as if it was a dangerous animal;

and frowning up at her.

"Just what is the meaning of this, Lesley?" he asked. His New England accent, not quite British, but close, was cold, as was his expression.

"Uh, well, sir," she said. "I saw a report about this in the intel traffic. I noticed that the embassy hadn't reported it, but, because of the implication that there might be foreign involvement, I thought they should look into it."

Whitman's expression got even colder. "You thought they should look into it? And, just what makes you think you have any business telling the embassy what they should be doing? Ambassador Ellingsworth is a capable Foreign Service Officer, and if he hasn't reported what is no doubt a minor incident, I'm sure he has his reason, and it's not for a mere desk officer to question him. Do I make myself clear?"

Lesley felt like crying, but held back the tears. She knew he'd expect her to do that. Whitman was one of the people who'd objected to her assignment, stating that a woman, and a consular officer at that, didn't have the necessary qualifications to perform well in the high stress environment of the country directorate. That had been, Lesley find out early on, total bullshit. While they worked often insane hours due to the time difference between Washington and most of the embassies with which they worked, the stress level was less than having to deal with a plane crash or a missing American whose relatives in the U.S. were constantly on the phone insisting that the U.S. Government find their kin, things that even the most junior consular officers had to learn to deal with very early in their careers. The desk officers read cables, wrote bullshit instruction cables, and wrote or cleared on even more bullshit memos for the various senior officials on the sixth and seventh floor of the State Department's C Street headquarters.

This, she thought, should have been just another routine request for additional information. The frosty look on Whitman's face, though, told her it was anything but. She'd done enough time behind visa interview windows, querying foreigners seeking visas to the United States, that she could spot deception with her eyes closed. Whitman was concealing worry; no, she thought; fear; behind his expression of frosty superiority. As he tore the green sheets, carbons included, into pieces and dumped them into the brown paper bag at the corner of his desk, the 'burn' bag into which classified trash was placed for incineration; she noticed that his hands trembled ever so slightly.

Something about the incident bothered him. Lesley Carter was determined to find out what, but decided not to press the issue with him.

"Yes, sir," she said, trying to put a tone of meek submission into her voice. "I just thought it might be useful, but, I see your point."

He nodded, looking at her from beneath his bushy brows. "Very well then; you have more important things to do, so I suggest you get to them. Where, for instance is that analysis of the crop production reports I asked for this morning."

"Uh, it's almost completed. I'll have it for you first thing in the morning."

This meant, she knew, that she'd have to take the files home and would be up all night drafting and redrafting.

She'd been working on it intermittently for most of the day, taking the occasional break to read items in the thick read file that circulated through the warren of tiny boxes that passed for office space for the half dozen desk officers she worked with. When she'd come across the intelligence report, it had piqued her interest; here at last was something besides boring columns of figures enumerating the hectares of wheat and other grains produced by the large state farms of Dagastan, outputs that were barely enough to feed its small population, requiring large shipments of grain and other foodstuffs from the country's Russian neighbors.

Dejected and disappointed by Whitman's reaction to her initiative to do something interesting, and to work on something that might actually have some political impact on U.S. relations with the tiny, insignificant country, she turned and with shoulders slumped, headed back to her tiny space; little more than a broom closet in comparison to the large corner office Whitman occupied. She would have been even more dismayed had she seen Whitman reach for the phone as she left; his narrowed eyes on her retreating back.

Back in her little cubbyhole, Lesley took the carbon copy of the cable Whitman had so casually dismissed and started to crumple it up to put in the burn bag. Then, she hesitated, looking at the purplish type on the green paper.

"No, dammit," she said quietly. "There's something here, and I'm getting to the bottom of it, one way or another."

She carefully smoothed out the single sheet and folded it in thirds. She put the folded paper in a legal size envelope, folded it in half and stuck it in her purse. Technically, she was about to commit a serious security violation, because, as was practice, she'd classified the cable CONFIDENTIAL, but she was so angry at the way she'd been rebuffed, she decided, to hell with it. No one checked employee purses on the way in or out of the State Department, and she could always burn it later.

She then took a sheet of plain paper and in her precise handwriting, wrote a short note. She folded the paper in half taped it, then put it in one of the brown interoffice envelopes used to ferry documents around the warren of hallways of the Department. Addressing the envelope to Alison Chambers, Central Asia Analyst, INR/ EUR, she got up and went outside. The secretary was bent over her desk, reading the Washington Post, and paid her no attention as she slipped the envelope into the stack of outgoing interoffice mail.

Back in her office, she spent the rest of the day making notations on the report Whitman had demanded. She was almost cheered up by the fact that she might actually be able to get most of it down before leaving for the day, alleviating the need to spend all night working on the damn thing.

When the hands of the circular clock mounted on the corkboard wall of her office were at six-fifteen, she removed the ribbon from her typewriter and locked it in the single drawer safe behind her chair, cleared her inbox of all papers, grabbed her purse, and, without looking around to see if anyone was noticing, left for the day. She had no doubt that some, if not all, the desk officers, all male, were sitting hunched over their desks watching the clock, waiting for a suitable 'late' hour to depart. She figured one or more of them would be making a mental note of her 'early' departure. The eight-to-five announced workday was a joke throughout the building. Only the civil servants who had permanent tenure could afford to actually work an eight-hour day.

To hell with it, she thought. The annual performance evaluations, the EERs, had already been done for the year, and she hadn't been in the section long enough to warrant a rating; she'd gotten a glowing evaluation from her last post, which would stand her in good stead when the summer promotion boards met beginning in June.

She was thinking about her prospect for promotion when the big red, white, and blue Metro bus pulled into the stop with a loud hiss of its air brakes, and the group on the sidewalk surged forward even before passengers getting off at that stop could exit the bus.

In the middle of the mass of people, Lesley managed to get on without being pushed around too much, and, luckily, snagged an inward facing seat near the front.

Sitting with her back against the wall, jammed in between a sweaty businessman who smelled of too many martinis with his lunch and an elderly black woman who was reading a dog-eared Bible, she kept her gaze fixed on the scuffed floor of the bus. She didn't notice, therefore, the quick glance she got from the man in black as he made his way past her to the back of the bus, where he stood, holding one of the overhead straps.

The L1 bus made its way up Twenty-third Street, around Washington Circle and onto New Hampshire Avenue, and then northwest on Connecticut toward Woodley Park and the National Zoo. By the mid-way point of the journey, and several stops where people got on, but few got off, the bus was crowded to capacity.

The twenty minute journey to Connecticut Avenue and Calvert Street, Lesley's stop, seemed like an eternity on the crowded vehicle with the smell of sweaty bodies and sweaty clothing assaulting her nostrils. The evening air, even with the mixture of gas fumes from all the cars roaring past on Connecticut, was a relief when she stepped down from the bus and headed up the hill toward the little town house she'd been able to rent a week after arriving in Washington for her assignment. Her air freight had arrived, but she was still waiting for her sea freight shipment, so the place was empty except for a card table and folding chair that did duty as dining surface and work space, and a futon upon which she slept. The few books she'd included in her limited air freight shipment were stacked neatly on the floor next to the futon, beside a gooseneck lamp she'd bought at a little shop in Bethesda. She hadn't bought a TV, so when she didn't spend the time before bed reading, she listened to a little transistor radio that her cousin had given her for her thirtieth birthday the previous year.

She was looking forward to getting inside her empty house; empty though it was, it was her territory, and she felt comfortable there, away from the pretense and coldness of official Washington.

She was completely unaware of the man in black, who had exited via the center door when she went out through the front, and was now trailing her, about twenty feet back. The sidewalk was deserted but for the two of them, and even at seven, the sky was still too light for the street lights to be turned on. Towering trees cast islands of deep shadow across the sidewalk. The man stayed as much in the shadows as possible, but it wasn't necessary, Lesley's attention was focused in front of her, and her destination, about half a mile farther along.

The dark stranger used the pools of shadow to close the gap between them, and it was only when he was no more than six feet behind her that Lesley Carter became aware of someone near; it was a feeling of sorts, the kind of itching tingle at the base of your neck that tells you that you're no longer alone. At first, she merely increased her pace. Only another hundred yards or so to go, and she would be inside her house; not, she thought, that she should really have anything to worry about. After all, Woodley Park was a nice area, populated by middle class families and professionals; not at all like some of the other DC neighborhoods where it was unsafe to wander out alone at night. It was probably just a neighbor, like her, coming home from a day of toil in some government office downtown.

It was after she'd made the turn up the side street on which her house stood that she began to have second thoughts about the sound of the footfalls behind her. They'd turned into the tree-lined narrow street that ended in a cul de sac three houses beyond hers moments after she had. She didn't know any of her neighbors, but couldn't recall any of them who would be coming from downtown at this time of day. Most were elderly retired couples who spent all day sitting on their porches or working in their tiny gardens.

She walked faster. Her house was now in sight, but the sidewalk, a dark gray blur in the shadows of the overhanging trees, seemed to stretch on forever. Her heart began to race, pounding in her chest like the native drums she'd heard during her visits to villages in Senegal. She clutched her purse against her small breasts and lowered her head. Could it be, she asked herself, a mugger? One of the lowlifes that infested the downtown areas, including the National Mall, preying on unwary tourists? If so, why was he so far out from town? She thought of the document in the folded envelope in her purse. What if he wanted her purse? Could she perhaps remove the money and placate him, thus not risking the incriminating document accidentally falling into the wrong hands?

The sound of the footsteps behind her was getting closer. Lesley wanted to run, but knew that her short, stocky legs weren't up to it. Suddenly, she felt the heat of anger and stopped in her tracks. The sound of footsteps stopped as well.

---

**_The White Dragon_ in paperback is available on most retail book seller sites. The Kindle version is available at Amazon.com and Amazon.uk.**

## Other books by this author:

**The Buffalo Soldier series:**

*Buffalo Soldier: Trial by Fire*
*Buffalo Soldier: Homecoming*
*Buffalo Soldier: Incident at Cactus Junction*
*Buffalo Soldier: Peacekeepers*
*Buffalo Soldier: Renegade*
*Buffalo Soldier: Escort Duty*

**Al Pennyback mysteries**

*Color Me Dead*
*Memorial to the Dead*
*Deadline*
*Dead, White, and Blue*
*A Good Day to Die*
*The Day the Music Died*
*Die, Sinner*
*Deadly Intentions*
*Death by Design*
*Till Death Do Us Part*
*Deadly Dose*
*Dead Man's Cove*
*Dead Men Don't Answer*
*Death From Unnatural Causes*
*Deadly Paradise*
*Kiss of Death*

**Other fiction**

*Angel on His Shoulder*
*She's No Angel*
*Child of the Flame*
*Pip's Revenge*
*Wallace in Underland*
*Further Adventures of Wallace in Underland*
*Dead Letter and Other Tales*
*The White Dragons*
*The Dragon's Lair*
*The Last Gunfighters*

**Nonfiction**

*Things I Learned from My Grandmother About Leadership and Life*
*Taking Charge: Effective Leadership for the Twenty-first Century*
*Grab the Brass ring*
*African Places: A Photographic Journey Through Zimbabwe and southern Africa*
*There's Always a Plan B*

# About the Author

**Charles Ray** has been writing fiction since his teens. He won a Sunday school magazine writing contest when he was thirteen, and having his byline on a short story published in a national publication forever hooked him on writing. During his time in the army (1962-1982) he often moonlighted as a newspaper or magazine journalist, and was the editorial cartoonist for the Spring Lake (NC) News, a weekly newspaper, during the 1970s. In addition to his writing, he was an artist/cartoonist and photographer for a number of publications, including Ebony, Eagle and Swan, and Essence, and had a monthly cartoon feature and did several covers for Buffalo, a now-defunct magazine that was dedicated to showcasing the contributions of African-Americans to the country's military history.

A native of Texas, he now calls Maryland home. For more on his writing and other projects, check one of the following Web sites:

http://redroom.com/member/charles-a-ray
http://charlesaray.blogspot.com
http://charlieray45.wordpress.com
http://www.twitter.com/charlieray45
http://www.facebook.com/charlieray45
http://www.flickr.com/photos/charlesray45/
http://www.viewbug.com/member/charlesray

www.ingramcontent.com/pod-product-compliance
Lightning Source LLC
Chambersburg PA
CBHW070904260626
47162CB00007B/2554

* 9 7 8 0 6 1 5 9 2 9 1 9 4 *